LAND SHARKS

A Swindle In Sumatra

OTHER BOOKS BY NANCY RAVEN SMITH

THE RELUCTANT FARMER OF WHIMSEY HILL

by
Bradford M. Smith

with
Lynn Raven and Nancy Raven Smith

Available Summer 2016

LAND SHARKS

A Swindle In Sumatra

(Book One of the Land Sharks Series)

by
Nancy Raven Smith

Whimsey Wylde
Santa Monica, California

Land Sharks

A Swindle in Sumatra

By Nancy Raven Smith

(Book One of the Land Sharks Series)

Published by Whimsey Wylde
Santa Monica, California

Printed in the United States of America

ISBN-13: 978-0988285842
ISBN-10: 0988285843

Cover Design: LimelightBookCovers.com

DEDICATION

For Brad
Who lives life with grace and love.
Who puts up with all my crazy ideas and who supports
me unconditionally. Thank you for making my life a joy.

AUTHOR'S NOTE

LAND SHARKS - A SWINDLE IN SUMATRA
is completely a work of fiction.
In no way does it reflect true events or real people.

CONTENTS

ACKNOWLEDGMENTS

I'd like to express my appreciation to the beta readers for Land Sharks: - Janice Metz, Judy Metz, Bobbi Knopf, and Terry Lynn Smith. To Barbara Kyle for sharing her expertise. To Masoud Parvis for giving me a peek into professional banking. To my writing teachers, Linda Palmer, Kate Wright, Neal Landau, Joe Bratcher, and Judy Farrell, for their generous sharing of knowledge. And warm thank you to the members of Sisters in Crime and the SINC Guppies for their support and willingness to answer all my questions.

I wish to thank the people of the Amazon/Kindle Scout Program and Kindle Press for offering a platform that gives writers a great opportunity to be seen by readers. And also for their great assistance from first to last with final editing and preparing Land Sharks for publication.

And a special thank you to Debi Smith, Terry and Jason Ebright, and Peter M. Smith for all their input, as well as my gratitude to my greater family for their unconditioned support.

I'm especially grateful to my parents, Francis and Marion Raven, for teaching me to love mysteries.

CHAPTER 1

Beverly Hills—where the scent of money is the must-have perfume and, like blood in the water, the slightest whiff attracts sharks.

At the moment, I'm eating at a trendy Asian fusion restaurant a block away from Rodeo Drive. My spicy shrimp dumplings and miso soup are excellent. I like the soup so much, I'm even wearing it dribbled down the front of my best white blouse. This is not an unusual occurrence for me. If restaurants would just supply bibs instead of napkins, I would save a lot on my cleaning bills.

Sadly, even in this nice restaurant, there is a nasty fish, and I don't mean on the menu. I'd classify him as a piranha. A piranha is a shark wanna-be. Those are my bread and butter . . . or more appropriately, my fish and chips.

This one is a young waiter named Bruce. He hasn't the

skills or the brains to ever move into the deep end of the pool with the real man-eaters, but he still needs to be stopped.

I watch as he accepts a credit card from one of three trophy wives seated in a window booth. The women wear the latest designer labels with their expensive boobs artfully semi exposed. At the moment, they are totally focused on checking out each other's baby shower gifts. Their irritating squeals of delight echo throughout the restaurant.

The woman paying for lunch will be making a different sound when she sees the next bill for the credit card she's handing him.

I first spotted Bruce skimming credit cards a week ago. It wasn't accidental. I was looking for him or someone like him after several of our bank customers complained of expensive, unauthorized charges on their cards. When I compared their statements, the only duplicate purchases I discovered were for charges at this restaurant.

I thought it would be worth a look to see if I could spot the thief. It wasn't hard. Bruce was so obvious he was easy to zero in on.

Normally, I would have turned him in to the police as soon as I spotted him, but he'd probably get off with only a slap on the wrist. So instead of reporting him, I decided to wait and see what Bruce did with the stolen information.

People like Bruce usually sell credit card data to buyers from identity theft rings for twenty to forty dollars each. The selling of personal identities has become so blatant that the thieves even advertise them on popular Internet sites. I have a hard time understanding why the police let them get away with that. I've seen lives that were destroyed by credit card theft.

The police can rarely help. Credit card fraud is at the bottom of their work list. Physical crimes against persons are their priority, and that keeps them busy twenty-four /seven.

In the last couple days, I've followed Bruce to his apartment on Fairfax, to his girlfriend's over the hill in Sherman Oaks, and to Puckett's Bar on Sunset where he plays pool incessantly. That's where I thought he'd hand off his skimmer, but no such luck.

The other person I'm watching in the restaurant is seated at the bar, reading the LA Times. I recognized him the minute he came in. Eddie Lee, aka Hong Kong Eddie. He's an impeccably dressed, hard-faced man of mixed Chinese heritage in his mid-thirties and wanted throughout Europe and the United States for credit card fraud. It's my job to be familiar with such con men because sooner or later they all come to try their hand in Beverly Hills. I think he may be Bruce's contact.

While I know him, he doesn't know me. I look like any other mid-thirties woman having lunch. Even my sandy-blonde hair is skinned back in a severe ponytail to make it unremarkable. I've been told I'm fashion challenged. In this case, my basic black suit is purposely not chic enough to be memorable. The only jewelry I have on is a pair of simple silver earrings and the small, antique silver cross pendant that I always wear.

Casually, Eddie lays down the newspaper and catches Bruce's eye. Bruce nods slightly as he passes, heading to the back room.

Bingo. I'm right. They are connected.

I watch Bruce ring up the bill for the baby shower woman. He glances around and then surreptitiously removes a small credit card skimmer from his pocket and slides the woman's card through it. Then he drops the skimmer into one of the restaurant's take-home bags.

Bruce crosses the room toward the table with the three women. He slides the take-home bag across the bar to Eddie and receives an envelope back. It could contain money or a new skimmer. It all appears innocent enough unless you know what you're looking at. Eddie drops some cash on the bar for his drink and leaves carrying the bag.

As he exits, I follow.

Eddie heads for Rodeo Drive. There, he threads his way through the constant parade of out-of-town lookie-loos ogling the display windows. I'll bet Rodeo Drive contains more greed, avarice, and just plain envy than any other street in the world.

Ahead of me, Eddie enters the posh Hermes store.

I slip into the shop behind him and pretend to be interested in some of their beautiful trademark silk scarves. Within minutes, Eddie's at the checkout counter with several silk ties, two pairs of diamond and ruby cuff links, and a crocodile skin briefcase. He hands the Hermes salesman an American Express credit card.

I can't see the total, but I know it has to be in the thousands.

The salesman rings up the purchases and asks Eddie for ID before running the credit card. Then he presents the receipt for Eddie to sign. "Thank you, Mr. Conklin. Please come again soon," he says as he wraps the items.

So it's a working day for Eddie, shopping with fake credit cards and ID. Excellent. He'll shop himself right into jail this time.

Next, Eddie, or should I call him Mr. Conklin, visits the Rolex shop where he purchases two men's Chronograph Daytona watches. This time, Eddie produces another fake ID and signs a Platinum Visa receipt.

The salesman says, "It was my pleasure to assist you, Mr. Johnson."

I trail Eddie as he makes big-ticket purchases in three more upscale stores, using a different credit card and ID in each—Huntsmeyer, Booker, and Whitmore. Retailers are also victims of identity fraud, but the card companies insure them against loss.

Just to be sure Eddie doesn't notice me, I change my appearance as we leave one of the stores. I remove my jacket as well as my hair clip, shake my hair down around my face, and add my sunglasses. Hopefully, the stains on my blouse won't look familiar.

He's halfway across the street at Rodeo and Brighton when the saleswoman from Bulgari, his last stop, erupts out of the store. She almost collides with me in passing.

She yells after Eddie, "Wait! Stop!"

I make a fast U-turn and duck into a doorway.

Eddie pauses, his body tense.

The saleswoman hurries toward him. "You forgot your receipt, Mr. Rashid."

"Uh . . . thank you."

"My pleasure. I hope you enjoy your purchases, Mr. Rashid."

I smile. That saleswoman chasing after him like that must have given Eddie a real scare. I dial my cell phone.

#

Hours later, and loaded with shopping bags, Eddie enters the swank Wilshire Boulevard Hotel. Outside his room, he removes the "Do Not Disturb" sign and inserts his key card in the slot. When the light flashes green, he shoulders his way into the dark room, letting the door shut behind him.

I note the room number and walk back toward the elevators to make a second call. I could probably kick the door in and go after Eddie myself to make a citizen's arrest, but there'd be a boatload of paperwork. I do have my Glock 17 with me. I'm just not fond of using it. Tonight, I'm content to let the police handle Eddie.

Ten minutes later, two Beverly Hills detectives exit the

elevator.

The first is Detective Jeff Corwin. In his mid-thirties, he still has the hard-muscled, tough body he got from being an amateur boxer in the Navy. His alert eyes quickly take in the area. They brighten when he spots me. At the same time, his mouth goes up in a crooked smile of greeting. I admit it. It's a great smile.

I give him Eddie's room number and point in the right direction.

Jeff and his partner, Gary Dutton, a former pro football linebacker, approach the door. Jeff knocks from a safe position beside it.

"Who is it?" calls Eddie.

"Police. Open up," says Jeff.

"Wait a minute." We can hear Eddie moving about in his room.

Jeff pulls his weapon. Gary braces himself, then smashes his shoulder into the door. It flies open.

Jeff steps into the room training his gun on Eddie.

At this point, I follow them in. I notice Eddie has thrown the hotel's satin comforter over something on the bed. I grab a corner and jerk it off, revealing an abundance of credit cards, watches, jewelry, cash, Nikons, passports, iPads, iPhones, laptops, and other small, expensive items. He's tried to kick the shopping bags from today under the bed, but some are only halfway hidden.

I point toward the bed. "Eddie, you've been a very naughty boy."

Gary quickly cuffs Eddie, giving him the "you're under arrest" spiel.

Jeff nods to me. "We picked up that waiter, Bruce, an hour ago."

"Thanks." Being a waiter or waitress is a hard enough job without crooks like Bruce giving them a bad name. At least he won't be ripping people off anymore.

"I wish this wasn't the only way we ever meet anymore," Jeff says.

"I do too." Jeff is a truly good guy. He's the one I should love. You could tell him your deepest, darkest secrets. Only, I can't burden him with mine. It wouldn't be fair.

"We're a long way from the academy," I manage.

"How about catching a bite after we run this guy in?"

"Jeff. . . . "

"Just remember, Lexi. I'm one of the few people who thinks you got railroaded."

I look away, struggling not to show how deeply his words touch me. Amazing how much my past still hurts.

"Okay, then," he says, obviously disappointed.

I can tell he's hoping for more from me, but it's all I have to share at the moment.

Behind Jeff, Gary shoots me a look of contempt. I know that look well. It's the one I normally get from law enforcement people who think they know my story.

"Call nine-one-one next time, not us," Gary says. "We're detectives, not your personal pickup service."

Eddie struggles as Gary hustles him to the door. Embarrassed, Jeff follows.

"Watch him closely. He's as slippery as they come," I say.

"He's a total waste of our time. You know he'll be out before morning," says Gary.

"Call Interpol. They want him," I say.

Gary shrugs.

Jeff turns. "If you'd stayed with the force, you'd be in homicide instead of chasing crummy credit card thieves."

"Eddie is not just some credit card thief. The money he sends back to his identity theft ring in Asia pays for human trafficking, guns, terrorism—you name it."

"So? The serious action's in Homicide," Jeff says.

I hold up a credit card. "People kill for these."

CHAPTER 2

I'm asleep on my office couch when a noise wakes me. Slowly lifting my nightshades from my eyes, I peer around my office.

It must be a false alarm. Nothing looks out of the ordinary. That is, unless you mistakenly consider the crumpled clothes on the floor or the dirty mugs, the open box of English breakfast tea, and last night's empty takeout cartons from the Chinese restaurant next door littering my desk as abnormal. They're not.

I never heard of a prize for cleanliness, so why bother? I've saved lots of energy for other things since I stopped wasting time on cleaning. My office may look messy, but I know exactly where everything is.

The sunlight peeks in under the drawn blinds. The angle of the light makes me think the sun's just rising. Downstairs, it's too early for the bank doors to be open to the public. I close my eyes. Unfortunately, it's not as easy to close my brain.

My office is pretty nice as offices go. The walls are painted a medium taupe color with white trim. The curtains and upholstery are silk and brocade in aqua, taupe, and teal patterns. Looking around, it makes me think about my career. I thought I'd enjoy being a policewoman, but even though I qualified, I found it didn't make me happy. I tried financial fraud investigation and discovered being a bank fraud investigator suited me perfectly. Since the police have their plates full, catching white collar criminals is an underserved field. That means the white collar criminals get to skate most of the time. I'm more than happy to have a small hand in stopping them.

The memory of taking down Bruce and Eddie yesterday makes me smile. I love it when a crook gets caught, especially by me. I'd probably do it for free if a paycheck wasn't necessary for paying the rent.

I roll over on the couch and pull the thick, down comforter up around my neck. Another fifteen minutes snooze won't hurt anything.

My doorknob rattles slightly, making my eyes fly open. That's the noise that woke me. I reach for my Glock hidden under my pillow.

There must be some employees about, but who would be trying to enter my locked office? It can't be a mistake because my name, Alexis Winslow, is clearly painted on the door.

There's the sound of a key sliding into the lock.

A key? Who has a key to my office?

I quickly flip myself over and behind the couch.

The door opens slowly.

It's only Steve Harrison. He's all of twenty-two and straight out of college. The epitome of a junior bank executive on the rise. Why he's in the Fraud Department, I have no idea. He'd be a great catch if you're into rich, attractive young men. At least he's harmless. I shove my gun out of sight under the comforter.

Steve glances over his shoulder to check if the corridor is empty. Shifting his coffee mug to his left hand, he enters, closing the door quietly behind him.

Thinking he's alone, Steve snoops through the clutter of papers on my desk. He finds one that interests him and reads.

I silently stand up. "Find what you're looking for?"

Steve jumps, spilling his coffee all over my papers. He grabs a box of tissues and tries to mop it up, managing to spread the spill over my entire desk.

"Come on. Don't you ever go home?" he says. "You need to get a life. If I was in charge, I wouldn't put up with the way you turned this office into a dump."

"You'll have to wait until you grow up and Daddy makes you head of his bank."

"I didn't get this job because Dad owns the bank. I graduated top of my class."

"And that gives you the right to break into my office?"

13

"I broke . . . .came in to leave you a note. Howard wants you."

"So why were you reading my report?"

"I . . . I—"

"Out. And leave that key."

"I can't. I have to return it to security."

I pretend to dig around under the comforter. "Where's my gun?"

He stops mopping, drops the key, and rushes for the door. He doesn't slow down as he disappears down the hallway.

I shake my head laughing. Steve can't really think I would shoot him. Still, he's a nuisance I don't need. He's one of two flies in my otherwise perfect job. His father, Morgan Harrison, the bank's president, is the other.

Fifteen minutes later, in my rumpled suit and fluffy rabbit slippers, I perch on a chair arm across from Howard Sutton, head of the Fraud Department. Steve sits nearby.

Howard is my immediate boss. He's way past retirement age, but while his sparse body may be weakening, his brain is still rapier sharp. They say he can walk into a room and smell a fraud. I don't doubt it. Rumor has it that he's former CIA.

I'm grateful for his being my mentor and supporter. Best of all, he forced Steve's father to hire me when I was desperate. I owe him dearly for that.

I glance from Steve to Howard with an unsaid question: "Why's he here?" Howard ignores me.

As I look, Steve crosses his knees so he's sitting exactly the way I am. Annoyed, I switch my legs. Steve immediately changes his position to match mine. They say imitation is the sincerest form of flattery, but really? The boy must be delusional if he thinks I'm worth emulating. I switch my legs again for the fun of it. Steve realizes I'm baiting him and his face turns a nice shade of pink. I could play this game all day.

Howard drops my soggy report on his desk. "I had no idea Eddie was in town. Nice job with him and that waiter. I appreciate that we're keeping good relations with the Beverly Hills police. However, I never want to see a report with wet coffee stains again. What does this last page say?"

Steve has the grace to squirm.

"I used one of the special credit cards with my name on it at the restaurant the first day I was there." Howard knows these are credit cards issued by our bank that appear normal. But if the card's used, it will alert the merchant that the user is a criminal to be reported to the police immediately. "I watched Bruce skim the card, so I guess we'll see who uses it if he passed it on before he got arrested."

"Where are you at the moment on the Michelsons?" Howard asks me.

"Still tracing the money he stole from his wife's trust fund before the divorce."

He shakes his head.

I can tell he doesn't think that's important. I know he only cares about cases involving millions, but two hundred thousand, give or take, is a huge amount and vital to Mrs. Mickelson. She's a newly divorced woman raising two small kids.

His intercom lights up and he answers it. Whatever the call is about, the frown on his face says it's not good news. He replaces the receiver without saying a word.

"I'll need that Mickelson research by this afternoon. Stay in the building and be available if I need you this afternoon." He looks over at Steve, "You, too."

That's it? I wonder what's going on for Howard to be so distracted. And what does Steve have to do with it?

I glance over at Steve. He looks totally pleased with himself. Whatever it is, it better not involve us working together. I stand and head for my office.

CHAPTER 3

On the way back to my office, Patricia, my favorite of the bank's vice presidents, catches me in the open hallway above the lobby. I have to hug her. She's the sweetest person in the whole world. The kind of person who manages to find good in everyone.

In her late forties and all of five feet tall in her bare feet, she has a penchant for six-inch stilettos and ultra-trendy clothes. Her gorgeous Latina black hair and flashing dark eyes make anything she wears look fabulous.

She holds out her left hand for me to see the enormous diamond she's wearing. Her smile is as brilliant as the gem. I'm glad to know that Conway, the man she's been going out with for the last couple years has stepped up to the plate. He's a nice guy and they're a perfect couple.

"So he finally did it. Congratulations." I kiss her on the cheek.

"I'm sure you'll find someone special and get married soon, too."

"I already did, but he left me." I bite my tongue. That just sort of slipped out of my mouth.

And it's news to Patricia. "You were married? What happened?"

"The usual. He ran off with another woman."

There's a commotion from the direction of the lobby below. Good thing. It distracts Patricia from any follow-up questions that I don't want to answer. We move to the railing and look down.

Below us, a thin, elegant man in his late forties motors his wheelchair across the main lobby, forcing his way between protesting groups of other people. He's Kevin Ochoa, the bank's biggest customer and best friend of the president since high school. Two bulked-up bodyguards follow in his wake. I met all three last year when I tracked a hacker for Kevin.

Both of his bodyguards are fiercely loyal to him. Mark Gaines is the older one. He's a savvy ex-marine. The other is Nate Tomlinson. In his late thirties, he's a guy who carries his testosterone as a badge of honor. He never met a woman he didn't try to grab. When you confront him about it, he acts like it's his right. I have to wonder if there are women anywhere that go for that approach. He should be made to wear a warning label: Toxic to Women.

"Kevin's got quite a scowl. He's not too happy about something," Patricia comments.

No, he's not. I wonder what's up. Could it be connected to the phone call Howard received?

We watch the scenario below as Steve's father, Morgan, hastens out to greet Kevin. There's a terse verbal exchange between them as they head into the conference room.

As the lobby settles down, Patricia gives me a hug and heads back to her office.

I look back down at the lobby. I notice a shirtless man whose name I don't know, but he comes in once a week to cash his paycheck. Today he's wearing camouflage pants, army boots, and has a six-foot boa constrictor wrapped around his neck like an accessory. Only one person below pays any attention to him or the snake. It's an older woman and she moves to the teller window farthest away. I'm not very fond of snakes either, but this one seems okay.

I smile and tell myself, it's LA, where people have no qualms about being individuals by showing their creative sides. It's one of the things I love about living here. I notice that Mary, the teller, doesn't even bat an eye as she chats with him and handles his transaction. Business as usual.

#

Twenty minutes later, I look up from my desk as Steve hurries in.

"Dad . . . I mean Mr. Harrison wants you in the conference room right away."

I slip into my good pumps and grab a legal pad.

With Steve on my heels, I thread my way between Kevin's bodyguards to reach the conference room door. I'm surprised when Nate doesn't call me "Foxy" or try to pinch my ass. Maybe he's sick today. Usually, he's such a jerk that he makes misogynist pigs look good. I don't get why Kevin puts up with him. Maybe he's an acquired taste.

Inside, Steve's father Morgan, Kevin, and Howard wait. For some crazy reason, they remind me of the three monkeys—hear no evil, see no evil and speak no evil. I stifle the thought quickly and suppress the smile that was creeping onto my face. I can tell from their expressions this is serious.

Before I can sit, Morgan asks me, "Is your passport in order?"

I nod. Out of the corner of my eye, I see Steve nod his head vigorously. What's with that?

"Good. Of course, you both know Kevin." Morgan's bulldog-like jowls flap as he talks.

Kevin and I shake as I slip into a chair. Steve steps over and shakes his hand.

"If I recall, you speak Indonesian?" Morgan continues.

"Only a little Bahasa. I think there are around two hundred and fifty other dialects."

"We want you to travel to Sumatra."

I panic and blurt out, "You know my Mom's not well. I don't want to be far away in case she needs me."

Morgan gives me a dismissive look. "Kevin has personally requested you," he says.

Alarmed, I start to stand.

He lifts a hand to stop me.

"Sit down. This is important. I don't want to hear any nonsense about your refusing to go out of the country when I need you. If I can't count on you, you're useless to me. I can easily hire someone to replace you"

I bite back the "I quit" teetering precariously on the tip of my tongue. He knows I'm trapped in this job. With my background, I can never get another bank job or qualify for a PI license. I'm such a bad cook that if I have to flip hamburgers for a living, all the customers will end up with food poisoning.

I glance around. Everyone looks at me expectantly.

Kevin cuts through the tension. "Please, Lexi. My daughter, Karista, left the country two days ago. I'm worried sick."

I have to admit he doesn't look well. His normally tanned face is drawn and pale.

"She apparently went of her own free will," Morgan says. "Howard tracked them last night. She and her new boyfriend. They landed at Singapore Airport and then flew on to Sumatra."

"Are the tickets round trip?" I ask.

"Yes, but they're open ended."

I look from one man to the other. "What am I missing?"

Kevin answers, "Karista and I had a big blow up over this man she's with. I had a bad feeling about him the minute I met him last week. He was evasive when I asked about his family and his background. As soon as they left, I had him investigated. He doesn't exist. Not under Javier Maynard, the name he gave. Nor is he a student at Stanford as he claimed. I called Karista to warn her, but she was so furious the minute she heard that I had him checked out that she hung up. Now she won't take my calls. I found out last night that she's quit school in the middle of the semester, and both of them are gone."

"They'll be back," Steve says. Kevin gives him a look that would freeze a hot potato.

"Why don't you just cut off her money? She'll have to call you," I say.

"That's the problem. I no longer control it. She just turned twenty-one. She's of age for the trust fund her mother left her."

I note Howard staring out the window. He's a smart man, and he's clearly not in agreement with Morgan and Kevin on this.

"If she just came into her own money, she's probably flaunting her independence," I say.

"That may be true, but I think it's more than that. Morgan just checked the funds in her account. There's already a large amount missing," Kevin replies. "I have to know if she's gone of her own free will or is being coerced. I can't sleep. I can't concentrate. I beg you to go and check it out for me. All you have to do is observe. Find out if she's being held against her will, then call me either way. I'll handle it from there. I won't be able to forgive myself if she's in trouble and I don't do anything. If I go to the police and Karista's just vacationing, she'll never speak to me again. They might even spook this Javier into doing something drastic. You can do it quietly. If she is in trouble, you can either get her away or I'll send in a hostage rescue team. Please, Lexi, say yes."

"Kevin is offering a nice bonus, plus all expenses," Morgan says. "Be ready tomorrow morning. Howard will have all the details."

In an effort to control my anger, I tune out his nasal voice and focus on the way his jowls flap when he talks. I glance at Howard. He's still staring out the window. It'd be nice if he helped me out here. Chasing wandering rich kids isn't part of my job description, which makes it an illegal request from an employer, but Morgan knows I won't file a grievance with the bank's board.

It's not my expertise, nor my job, but there's no answer I can give in the face of Morgan's threat to fire me and Kevin's obvious pain.

I swallow my fears and say, "Yes, of course, I'll go."

CHAPTER 4

Two hours later, I can't keep my eyes open. The airport security videos Howard managed to acquire have been a waste of my time. The pictures are grainy and were installed at terrible angles.

Not one single camera from any vantage point anywhere got a clear shot of Javier. He wore a hat and wrap-around sunglasses in both airports. His forceful body movement suggested he's arrogant and impatient.

Karista, on the other hand, is a beautiful young woman with all the polish and snobbery of a rich girl who grew up in Beverly Hills. She never spoke to anyone except Javier and managed to avoid eye contact with people as she walked, making her look like a real snob. Not an unusual result of having lots of money. She also wore her sunglasses constantly in the airports. I guess the fluorescent airport lighting hurt their eyes. Arrogant and snobby. Quite the lovely young couple.

I slam my pad on my desk in annoyance. Why can't Morgan just leave me alone? How dare he order me on this job like some flunky? I have my reasons for passing up trips outside the country. I love foreign travel, but not right now.

All for this fool's errand. Kevin admitted he took Karista with him on a business trip to Indonesia a few years ago. She'd loved the area. If that's true, then her returning there makes it look like a simple vacation.

I never met Karista. She was away at school when I worked with Kevin, but the pictures of her all over his house and his office were hard to miss. Her mother died in a car accident right after she was born, so it's been just the two of them all her life. I get that they're close. Those photographs showed a pretty young girl with her whole future ahead of her.

Of course she has a boyfriend. What young man wouldn't be attracted to her? And what father doesn't dislike his only daughter's boyfriends? Though the fake name and the lies sound serious. Gold-diggers and scam artists circle rich people like vultures. It must be hard to be a young person going through life questioning every relationship. Does he love me, or my money?

I'm not sure what to think. Karista's boyfriend could just be some nervous guy making up stuff to date a pretty girl he likes.

Kevin's a nice man. I do feel for him. Raising a kid on

your own these days can't be easy, but in the absence of a ransom demand his paranoia seems ridiculous.

Howard knocks and enters, interrupting my thoughts.

"Thanks for the help," I say.

He lifts a hand to shush me before I can go off on what I think of him, Morgan, and this whole situation.

"It doesn't matter. It's an international case."

"And we all know how well my last case abroad went."

He ignores me. "I don't ever want to hear that bs about your Mother again. We both know she's healthy and living the good life in Florida.

Oops. I forgot he does regular check-ups on the bank's staff.

He continues, "And we both know the real reason you're reluctant to leave the country. You need to get over it."

"But I. . . . "

"No buts. You have the most experience and Kevin wants you. It won't hurt to have him in our debt."

"Does it matter what I want?" Apparently not. He changes the subject.

"Kevin called his daughter's roommate, Denise Boyd, as you requested. She wasn't in, but he left a message with the housekeeper."

"Housekeeper?"

"Karista doesn't live in a dorm. Kevin bought a house near the school for her. It gives her room for her artwork."

"How nice."

"Here are the tickets for this afternoon's commuter hop to San Francisco. I made arrangements for a limo to be waiting at the airport to drive you down there."

He drops a briefcase on my desk. I don't like that he hasn't met my eyes since he came in.

"Morgan thinks this whole thing is a proverbial fool's errand, but he's going through the motions for Kevin's sake. He says the girl's got too much money and too few brains."

"That mixture is a known recipe for disaster."

He nods. "I have an uneasy feeling about this. It won't hurt for you to go, but just observe and get out quickly. It shouldn't take more than a couple days. Remember, you'll have no status there and no back up."

I've learned to listen to Howard's intuition, but he seems evasive. I wonder what's going on. "Why not hire someone who's an expert in international kidnapping recovery? They're all over the Internet. I'm sure you know a few personally. This is totally out of my expertise. Are you even listening to me?"

He stares out the window.

"Is there something you're not telling me?" I ask.

"Sorry, I just have a lot on my mind."

That's a weak excuse. Howard has a mind like a computer. A lot on his mind doesn't affect him like it does the rest of us. Is he lying to me? I don't think he's ever done that before.

"What if I screw up again?"

He ignores me and indicates the briefcase. "Inside are tickets for Sumatra. You'll leave tomorrow morning. You can pick your visa up when you land in Sumatra. There's a kiosk in the airport."

"A satellite phone?"

"You'll have it in the morning before you leave. Also, there's some precautionary shots you should take. The doctor said it would have been better to take them earlier, but better late than never." I made the arrangements. Get them before you head up to Stanford.

"Howard, I . . . Howard, Kevin has no right to entrust the safety of his daughter to me. I can't even take care of myself."

"He said all he wants you to do is observe. You can do that." He waves me off.

I bite back my objections. Maybe there will be no problems. Especially if there's nothing wrong with Kevin's daughter. Like Howard said, it could be a pretty quick trip.

Howard continues, "I made reservations for both of you at the Star of Sumatra Hotel where Karista made reservations on her credit card."

"Wait. . . . Both?"

He gives me a funny smile. "Since Morgan thinks this is a low-risk trip, he's decided to send Steve along with you for experience."

"No. Absolutely not. I didn't agree to that. You know I only work alone."

"Come on. The boy won't learn if we don't teach him."

"Very noble, Howard. Why don't you teach him?"

"Because I outrank you."

Point taken. There's no arguing with that.

"Lexi, go easy on Steve. He just might surprise you."

CHAPTER 5

Three hours later and feeling like a pincushion after receiving the required shots, Steve and I are in the limo speeding south on interstate two-eighty to Palo Alto to see Karista's roommate, Denise.

"I'm hoping she can tell us more about Javier," I say.

"I asked Howard to update me on the job, but he said it would be better if I hear it from you," Steve says.

"I bet he did."

There's not much Steve didn't hear in the meeting, so filling him in is brief. I stress that Kevin doesn't want his daughter to know he's checking up on her. When we get to Sumatra, we're not to introduce ourselves as employees of her father or the bank. We're just American tourists who happen to be vacationing at the same hotel. There's to be absolutely no police involvement. He wants to keep her record clean. If we discover she has been kidnapped, we call Kevin.

"Do you think—"

"No, I don't. All indications appear like they went away for a vacation. Your father thinks Kevin's overreacting."

He looks disappointed, but I don't mention Howard's suspicions.

Before long, we turn off at Sand Hill Road in Palo Alto. We make a few more quick turns near Stanford University before the limo pulls up in front of a lovely, pale yellow stucco house with dark wood trim. I can see the edge of a pool in the back. I get a flashback to the tiny apartment I shared at college with three other girls. The closest thing we had to a pool was a dirty shower stall.

Steve rings the doorbell. When the door opens, we're confronted by a six-foot tall woman with bulging biceps and tattoos of dragons up both arms. I definitely wouldn't want to climb in a wrestling ring with her.

"I'm Sherry," she announces. "You the people Kevin sent?"

When we nod, she leads us into the living room. The rooms we can see are tastefully done by a professional decorator in cream, apricot, and cinnamon. I wonder if the decorator was hungry when he picked the colors.

Sherry disappears into the kitchen and returns with a tray of coffee and cookies. "I made them this morning."

I'm liking Sherry. Where was she when I went to school?

Steve and I dig in.

"Thanks," Steve says. "I'm starving."

She beams at him.

"Is Denise in?" I ask.

I take a sip of coffee. Yikes. It would strip the paint off an aircraft carrier. I add as much cream as I can get into the cup.

"I haven't seen her for the last couple days, but the girls and I have an agreement. They like their privacy, so I don't go up to the second floor except on Mondays with the cleaning crew. I did call and leave a message on Denise's cell that you were coming. I heard it ring upstairs, but she didn't pick up."

Out of the corner of my eye, I see Steve take his first taste of the coffee. I watch as his eyeballs roll. He manages to stop them mid-roll. Surprisingly, he grins at Sherry. "Great coffee. Thanks."

The boy does have manners.

Sherry smiles and urges him to take a cookie.

I cut in, "Before we check with Denise, would you mind answering a few questions?"

"Kevin said you were to have anything you wanted, so I guess that includes questions."

Steve bites into the cookie and a look of pleasure crosses his face. Sherry's smile widens, enraptured with him.

I try to get her attention. "Did you ever meet Javier?"

"Oh yes. That man is here so much, Karista should

33

charge him rent. Nice guy, but odd."

"In what way is he odd?"

Sherry pauses. "It's kind of hard to pinpoint. He's quiet and doesn't talk a lot, but that's okay with me."

Hmm. Nice and quiet. Isn't that the same thing that the neighbors say about every serial killer after he's been caught?

"And he might be a hypochondriac," Sherry continues. "He always had one of those antiseptic wipes in his hand."

I ask, "Do they get along? Does he treat her well?"

"He dotes on her. Flowers at all hours for no reason at all. Candy, gifts. Out late to clubs and tickets for concerts all the time."

"They ever argue?"

"I've never seen them disagree. It's Karista and Denise that had a big fight about Javier back when they first started dating. Denise said he came on to her a couple times."

I choke on my cookie. It's as bad as the coffee. Steve slaps me on the back and grins. I glance at Steve with annoyance. He snickers as he bangs me on the back again.

"Must have gone down wrong," I manage to mumble.

"Did you see Javier come on to Denise?" Steve asks Sherry.

"No, not that I ever saw. I think maybe Denise stepped over the line with Karista by accusing him. She thinks he can do no wrong."

"Did Karista believe Denise?" I ask.

"No. I heard Javier tell her it was the other way around. Denise came on to him. Of course, if he says the moon is green, she'd believe him. He and Denise never did get on after that. In fact, Karista even mentioned she was thinking of asking Denise to move out."

"Do you know how they met?"

"Probably over on campus."

Not much help.

"Is there any article in the house that Javier was the last one to touch?"

She thinks a minute. "Maybe in Karista's room. Wait. You're thinking fingerprints aren't you? What's going on here? Is Karista—"

"Karista's fine."

"As far as we know," adds Steve. I shoot him a look.

"What's going on here?"

"Kevin likes to know who Karista's dating," I say. "Nothing more."

I can tell Sherry's not sure if she believes me, but she stops asking questions..

"Were you here two days ago, when he and Karista left?" I say.

"No. I was at a friend's place. We were making the cookies for our book club the next night. When I came home, it was late. I went straight to my place. I live in the guest house out back."

"What exactly are your duties?" I ask.

"Supervise the cleaning crew on Mondays, keep the

kitchen stocked, cook, drive for the girls on occasion, bounce unwanted boyfriends, and step in if any of their parties get unruly."

"How did Karista seem? Was she happy about the trip?"

"Must have been. Had herself a big old shopping trip the day before. New dresses and sandals. Oh, and a huge, yellow sun hat."

"Thanks. I guess we should check with Denise now. If you don't mind, we may have a few more questions before we leave."

Sherry picks up the phone and dials. We can hear her ringtone, "The 1812 Overture," play faintly from upstairs. "She's not picking up, but that's her phone. Maybe she's in the shower."

"Can we go up and knock? I'd like to take a look at Karista's room, too."

"Denise is first door on the right. Karista's on the left. Second door on the left is Karista's work room. I can get that tray for you."

Sherry gathers the dishes and heads to the kitchen. Steve and I climb the hall stairs.

I whisper, "Why didn't you warn me about the cookies?"

"Like you warned me about the coffee?"

He continues, "Sherry went to a lot of effort for us. I didn't want to hurt her feelings.

Drat. I hope Steve isn't going to turn out to be a nice

guy. I would hate to be forced to like him.

We enter Karista's room first. It's in disarray. Empty shopping bags from Neiman-Marcus and Bloomingdales are shoved in one corner. Bureau drawers hang open with clothes spread out on the chair and bed. The down comforter still has the square imprint of a suitcase.

I nose around a bit. Cosmetics and toothbrush missing from the bathroom. School books stacked on the desk. A large portfolio leans against the wall. I open it. Inside are some elegant fashion designs she's done. I'm impressed. Karista has a lot of talent.

I move on to the walk-in closet. Shoes are scattered all over the floor. Clothes hang half on and half off the hangers. In other words, except for the drawings, it's a typical well-to-do student's room for someone who just left on a trip. I was hoping for a photograph of Karista with Javier. I'm surprised not to see any.

As we're leaving, I check out the trash can. Lots of receipts and discarded mail, including credit card bills and bank statements. All the information identity thieves love. Kevin needs to buy his daughter a shredder.

Shoved under the bills is an empty silver picture frame with a cracked glass. Not good. I hand it to Steve. "Run this by Sherry. I'd like to know what was in it." He heads downstairs with it.

I pop into Karista's work room. It's bright and sunny, a good place for doing her artwork. Where her bedroom is a mess, this room is well organized. Canvases stacked against one wall in vertical shelves. Oil paints, brushes, and charcoals in separate shallow bins on the counter. I pull a few of the canvases out. The paintings are upbeat and well executed.

I notice computer plugs and a printer on her work desk, but the computer is missing. She probably took it with her. There are no photographs of Javier in this room, either.

As I'm exiting, Steve rejoins me.

"Sherry said it was a recent picture of Karista and Javier at a night club."

That's what I was afraid of. Not good that there are no pictures in the house of Javier. What young girl, or even older woman, doesn't moon over pictures of herself with her boyfriend?

"Too bad the computer's gone. She might have his picture posted."

"Maybe she posted his picture on social media, like a selfie with him."

"Good idea."

Hopefully, Denise will be able to tell us what we need. We head for her room. There's no answer when I knock on her door. I test the knob. It's not locked. I step inside.

"Wait. Should we...?" Steve asks.

Too late. I'm in.

"Hello? Denise? Karista's father sent us. Can we talk with you?"

I look around. My skin prickles. Something's not right. A lamp and a chair lay on the floor. Unlike Karista's room, which looks simply messy, this room looks like a fight took place in it. Things are turned over, cushions are on the floor. I notice the contents of a woman's purse dumped all over the bureau. Wallet, keys, lipstick, and her cell phone.

"Denise?"

I caution Steve to stay at the door in case she is in the shower. I check the room and then the adjoining bathroom. The shower is dry. No Denise.

I open the closet. Nothing but clothes on the shelves above, but when I push the clothes apart. My hand goes reflexively to the silver cross on my necklace.

It's Denise.

She won't be answering our questions tonight.

She's dead. Her throat slit.

CHAPTER 6

After we call, the police show up in less than ten minutes. The detectives come in right behind them. They immediately separate the three of us into different rooms for questioning. Too late. We've already coordinated our stories. Poor Steve. He's freaked out about Denise. Me, too. Thank goodness he couldn't see her body from the doorway.

I can't stop thinking about Denise, either. Sherry said she was sweet, well liked, and a bit naive. And that she had appeared particularly happy lately. So why would anyone want to hurt her in such a horrific way? With a knife?

I'm having a hard time not heaving up the contents of my stomach. It's not that this is my first dead body, but I'll never get used to murder. Especially a young girl with her throat slit.

I have a deadly fear of knives. I even have nightmares

about them. I was accosted in Brisbane once by a druggie wielding a knife. He'd already killed one person. I might not be here today if the person I was with hadn't shot him in the nick of time. Late at night, I still see my face transposed on the body of the woman the druggie had killed earlier.

It was a good thing I'd already made a career change to bank investigator before that happened. Police women aren't much good if they're afraid of knives.

Since then, I can't bear to have any knives in my apartment, even kitchen knives. The only one I own is a butter knife. I use scissors to cut things. Scissors might be just as dangerous, but my brain doesn't react to them the same way. Fortunately, I live on takeout, most of which is bite-size.

I won't tell Morgan and Kevin that if I find that Karista and her boyfriend are involved, I'm going to be first in line at the police station with any information that helps them get a conviction. If Morgan fires me after that, too bad. I didn't know Denise, but she didn't deserve this.

Steve and I had nothing to do with Denise's death. I can't imagine Sherry did, but waiting alone in this room for the detective gives me terrible flashbacks of two years ago when my entire future was on the line, and it didn't go well. This time, like that one, I'm completely innocent, and yet my hands are shaking. Clasping them tightly, I unsuccessfully try to force them to stop. If this detective checks to see if I have a record, he may give me a rough time. I'd do anything to get that spot off my record.

After a long thirty minutes, a man enters the room with a notebook and introduces himself as Detective Robert Burton. Older and slightly unfit for a cop, he must be near retirement age. I make an effort to appear calm.

"Now then, Ms. Winslow."

"Lexi, please."

He ignores me. "I understand you discovered the body. How did you know Denise Boyd?"

"I didn't."

Burton is surprised.

"Then why were you in her room?"

"My coworker, Steve, and I flew up today with some papers for Karista Ochoa to sign."

"You flew up just for a signature? Wouldn't a fax or FedEx be a lot cheaper?"

"We work in a small bank. Karista's father is one of our biggest customers. We offer him every courtesy. Steve is a new employee, so he's along for training."

Burton doesn't appear convinced.

"You're saying no one bothered to call and find out if Karista was here?"

"We had a confirmed appointment. It didn't seem necessary."

"And yet, she's not here."

"She's young. I guess a vacation was more exciting than signing documents. She just forgot to cancel. The bank will charge a fee for our trip."

"In other words, she's a rich kid who doesn't care about inconveniencing others. Like all these other college kids around here."

Normally, I'd contradict him. Most young people today are conscientious and smart. Of course, the jury is still out about Steve, but I want to get through this interview and out of here. The Palo Alto police can't touch Karista and Javier in Sumatra, but I can. If she's innocent, then she could be in danger from Javier if he killed Denise. No telling what could happen to her while she's so far from home. Is that why Javier took her out of the country? Because she was a witness?

I have too many questions, but first I need to make sure I'm not held here as a witness or arrested. Someone needs to get on that plane tomorrow and get to her quickly.

"If you're here to see Karista, why were you in Denise's room?" Burton asks.

"To see if Denise knew when Karista would be back."

Uh oh. It dawns on me that I have no excuse for opening Denise's closet. I can't even think of a believable reason. If he asks that, I'm in trouble.

"Do you have the ticket for your flight?"

I pull it from my pocket and hand it to him.

"And these papers you wanted Miss Ochoa to sign? Where are they?"

"In my briefcase."

"Let's see them."

"They're personal. You'll need a warrant."

He doesn't like that at all.

"Sit tight. I'm going to make some calls. I'll be right back."

I'd already made a quick call to Kevin and Howard while we waited for the police to arrive. They agreed to confirm the prearranged meeting story. No problems there, but I can only hope that Steve and Sherry stick to it. Contrary to most television shows, police are well schooled in detecting inconsistencies in what they're told.

I'm forced to wait a long time while Burton confirms my story. I try to focus on just breathing in and out. After a bit, there's a murmur of voices outside the room. I move to the door and open it a crack.

I hear the medical examiner telling Burton that it looks like Denise was killed with some kind of curved or serpentine knife about forty-eight hours ago.

Not good. That's the day Karista and Javier left. I close the door silently.

Moments later, Burton enters and returns my plane ticket.

"You and your partner are free to go." It comes out tensely. I can tell he hates saying it.

"Thank you," I get up quickly and leave the room, successfully cutting off any "Don't leave town" add-on that might be coming.

I pass the room where Sherry is answering questions for another detective. Poor Sherry, he's leaning over her like a vulture. I can hear the fear and shock in her voice.

"Do you truly expect me to believe that in two days you haven't been upstairs?"

"I told you, we have this arrangement. You should be checking if Karista and her boyfriend are okay."

Burton comes up the hallway behind me, forcing me to move on into the living room. He enters the room with Sherry and closes the door. That's okay. I can't get away from here quickly enough. My stomach is in a knot.

I'm glad Kevin is on his way up with his lawyer to help her. I've asked him to do three important things. Check the tray Sherry mentioned for Javier's fingerprints. Find out if there's a picture of Javier on Denise's phone or anywhere else and run it through facial recognition. That failing, put Sherry with a sketch artist and see if she can come up with a likeness of him.

Steve waits in the living room like a zombie. I indicate the front door, and we're back in the limo in a heartbeat. He looks as torn up as I feel.

"When we get back, check with Kevin. See if he has access to Karista's social media. Look for the boyfriend. Try to get on Denise's sites, too. Maybe there's a group picture. Did your detective say anything to you about not leaving the country?"

He spots my trembling hands.

"Are you all right?" he asks.

"I'm fine," I lie. I turn to the Driver. Please let's go." I don't want the detectives to see me blow lunch.

CHAPTER 7

Getting up at dawn after three hours of sleep and managing to arrive at LAX to catch the first of the several flights I need to reach Sumatra feels like a major accomplishment. Poor Denise was even in my dreams. I order the strongest espresso I can at the airport's coffee bar. Maybe I'll stay awake long enough to board and find my seat.

Before arriving at the airport, there was a hasty meeting at the bank, followed by collecting all the necessary paperwork and the sat phone from Howard.

One good thing happened. Morgan withdrew Steve from the trip. He decided that with Denise's death, it was too dangerous to let him go. Steve was livid. He accused his father of having a double standard where he was concerned. I agree with Steve. If it's too dangerous for his son, why is it okay for me to go?

Kevin insists he wants me there for Karista. He says he trusts my judgment of the situation. I did manage to extract a promise that he'd send in a professional recovery team if I determine that Karista's in danger.

That's fine with me. I don't fancy a shoot-out with a kidnapper. Especially since I have no way of getting a weapon on a plane and through customs without a lot of explanations to the local authorities.

I finish my espresso as I wait my turn at the security check point. The line moves forward until I can toss my shoes and my carry-on bag onto the conveyor for the scanner. My espresso cup goes in the trash.

I hear a commotion behind me. It's Steve. What's he doing here?

He's dressed in some banana republic version of tropical jungle chic that he doesn't have the maturity to carry off. The fancy camera slung around his neck doesn't help. All he needs to complete the outfit is a pith helmet. On the plus side, he does look exactly like an American tourist. Should I give him points for that? Nah, it wouldn't do to spoil him.

He waves from the back of the line. Great.

He catches up with me at the boarding gate and sits beside me.

I have to ask. "I thought your father—"

He holds up his ticket. "He did. I'm an adult. I can make my own decisions."

They call boarding for our flight. I stand and move into

line. Steve follows.

"Look, Steve. Your father's right. You might want to sit this one out. It could get nasty."

"Then you should have someone with you. End of story."

He surprises me. No one's ever said that to me before. I've always worked alone, so it's not that I need someone, especially not someone who is wet behind the ears and will need to be protected. Still, the sentiment is nice. I give up and hand the agent my boarding pass. After all, he is an adult.

When the plane finally lifts off, I settle back with a glass of champagne. I could really get to like this first class stuff. Working for Kevin does have its merits. Morgan never springs for first class. The comfy seat and the alcohol ease some of the claustrophobia I normally get flying coach. This part's going to be fine. It's the rest of the trip that has me worried.

"So what's our plan?" Steve asks.

"My agenda is different than Kevin's and your dad's. I want to know if Karista and Javier are involved with Denise's death."

"The timing's not auspicious."

"I know. Best case scenario is that Karista's not involved and we bring her home safe."

I have a sudden bad thought. "Karista doesn't know you, does she? I mean your Dads are old friends."

"Last time I saw her was at her sixth or seventh

birthday party. There's no way she'd ever recognize me," Steve says.

I hope that's true. Otherwise it would certainly blow our cover. "Remember, she'll be familiar with the name Steve Harrison. You're Steve Winslow, and we're relatives."

"You don't really think she could be involved, do you? It has to be that boyfriend of hers."

I shake my head. "We'll see. Did you get people started on Karista's and Denise's social media?"

"Howard's working on it. Both their sites were canceled recently. Have you been to Sumatra before?" Steve asks.

"Ages ago to Java, but not Sumatra."

"Me neither. Should be fun."

Fun's not the word I'd use to describe this trip.

He pulls out a guidebook on Indonesia and settles back to read.

"I don't know if your guidebook mentions it, but when you break the law in Indonesia, they bring out a firing squad and execute you."

CHAPTER 8

Steve and I get a beautiful view of Sumatra as our plane circles during the approach to Kuala Namu International Airport, just outside the city of Medan.

It looks like a scene from Steve's travel book. Black smoke pours from the Mt. Sinabung volcano. "It's one of a hundred and thirty active volcanoes in Indonesia," Steve points out. "And there's Lake Toba glistening like a jewel, just like the guidebook describes it. Did you know the Toba volcano has produced the largest eruptions on earth in the last two million years?"

No, I didn't.

"And Sumatra has tigers, elephants, and tapirs? And thousands of bird species?" Steve reads from his guidebook.

"Let's hope we're not here long enough to meet any of the tigers."

We pick up Steve's large red bag at the luggage carousel, pass quickly through customs, and traverse the teeming airport, heading for the exit. Steve tries to appear nonchalant and still absorb the exotic humanity around him. That's hard for him to achieve while dragging his large suitcase, and matching carry-on bag behind him. I've learned over the years that one carry-on is best for travel, especially these days.

"Did you read about the boogey men in your guidebook? You want to be on the lookout for them."

"Come on. That's just something people say to scare little children."

I look at him knowingly, but don't answer—making him unsure. I wonder if teasing him will become my new sport. No. It's too easy. It has the feel of picking on a baby lamb. Even I wouldn't sink that low—would I?

We move through a crowd of brightly attired Muslims, Hindus, Buddhists, Merapus, and other Indonesians mixed with a scattering of Europeans.Steve's eyes follow a beautiful young Balinese woman in native dress and he runs smack into a tattooed Dayak warrior wearing a beaded, and feathered headress.

Steve freaks. "Excuse me . . . I'm so sorry. I wasn't looking."

He would have had reason in the past to be frightened. The Dayak people from Borneo were known for their traditional headhunting activities. Now most are Christian or Muslim.

The warrior notices the Balinese woman and says in articulate British English, "It's quite all right. You will find much beauty in Sumatra."

I pass a barefoot beggar with decaying teeth standing inside the door. He eyes Steve's expensive-looking baggage. I observe him exchange a look with a cute, well-dressed young woman in her late twenties nearby. The woman sips her coffee and watches Steve with calculation.

We emerge from the airport onto the sidewalk and are assailed with a one-two punch. First our bodies hit a wall of heat and unbearable humidity. Second, our ears ring from an overwhelming cacophony of noise. Suddenly we're surrounded by porters in yellow jumpsuits. All vying for our business. I wave them away.

The sidewalk is packed with people, and the dense street traffic is a sea of vehicles. Minibuses, cabs, bicycles, cars, and becaks, the Indonesian version of tricycle pedicabs. There's even a horse cart or two, but nothing we can identify as our hotel transportation.

"Check that way. Someone should be here from the hotel," I tell Steve.

I go to the right and am immediately swallowed by the surging crowd. After a minute, I turn back to see if Steve's having better luck in his direction.

I manage to catch glimpses of him in the distance. He's put his bags down to wipe the sweat from his forehead. Bad move. His eyes and hands aren't on his luggage.

I spot the young woman who's connected to the beggar

inside the airport step out of the crowd behind Steve and deliberately bump into him, spilling her coffee down his shirt. Alarmed, I race in his direction.

"Oh, Monsieur. Pardonez moi. I am so sorry," the woman says to Steve.

He's fascinated as her flitting fingers move around his jacket, trying to mop up the mess with her handkerchief.

"Please. It's nothing."

"You are so kind. Allow me. I am so clumsy."

"Really, it's—"

"It was so bad of me. Your poor coat is ruined. It was all my fault. Please, tell me that you forgive me."

"I can have it cleaned." Steve catches sight of the beggar's back as he races away with his red luggage.

"Hey, you. Stop. Stop thief!"

The beggar only runs faster, weaving in and out of the crowds on the sidewalk.

Steve sprints after him, but the beggar has too big a lead. He pulls away, heading straight toward me.

When the beggar comes close I stick my foot out. He trips end-over-end and drops Steve's bags. I'm reaching for his collar when someone collides with me from behind. We both go down on the pavement, and I lose my grip.

I turn to confront my attacker.

It's Steve.

I turn back to the beggar. Too late. The beggar scrambles to his feet, grabs the closest of Steve's bags, and disappears into the crowd.

Steve apologizes, "I couldn't stop in time,"

"I hope your mother packed your clean underwear in the other bag."

Steve grabs his remaining bag. "Rats. He got my new Nike Red October Air Yeezys."

"Seriously? Your shoes have a name? Yeezys?"

"They're extremely special. A man from Michigan even tried to trade a pair of rare Addidas Yeezys for a new kidney."

"Did someone really take him up on that?"

"I never heard."

I shake my head. "Well, yours are long gone."

Steve ignores me. "I was talking to this French woman—"

I point to the spot on his coat. "Yes, I saw. The one who spilled the drink on you."

"It was an accident."

"Don't you know anything?"

He doesn't understand.

"You were tag-teamed. She distracted you, he grabbed your bags."

"That's crazy. She was well dressed and nice. There's no way she was in cahoots with that beggar."

"Think about it, Steve. Where is she now?"

He looks around. There's no sign of the French woman. He feels his pocket. "My wallet. It's gone."

"Did they get your checkbook?"

He nods. "We should report them to the proper

authorities."

"Your passport?"

"No. It's under my shirt like you told me."

"That's lucky. This is a really bad place to lose personal documents." The area is the world's crime hub for fake and stolen travel and financial documents. Sixty thousand stolen passports disappear just north of here in Thailand in one year so glue your passport to your body if you have to."

"I should report it."

"Forget it. Your girlfriend's long gone. Let's not attract any more attention, okay? You can cancel your cards from the hotel."

"Please don't tell Dad I screwed up already."

I try to take the sting out. "Come on. We can call Howard. He can deal with it without telling Morgan."

We wait another hot, sweaty hour before I spy a jeep with the name Star of Sumatra Hotel on the side. When I catch the driver's attention, he heads in our direction and stops. Steve helps him toss our bags into the jeep.

I start to get in, then realize someone else is in the back seat. I freeze.

No. It can't be. Not the one man in the universe I hoped never to see again and the reason I was arrested two years ago. What on earth is he doing here in this remote place? Surely it can't be a coincidence.

He's Andre Van der Meer and I hate to admit it, but he still takes my breath away. You wouldn't call him handsome, but there's an undeniable appeal about him. Maybe it's the twinkle in his eyes or his smile that goes higher on one side than the other. He must be thirty-six by now. Definitely the kind of suave, engaging European every woman in the world dreams she'll meet. He's wearing a safari jacket that looks as natural on him as stripes on a tiger. And I know he's just as attractive in a Savile Row suit or even without . . . no, I refuse to go there.

But women aren't the only ones who'd like to run into him. The FBI, the CIA, and Interpol, in particular, would pay to know his whereabouts. Too bad my sat phone is in the bottom of my carry-on bag in the back of the jeep. I programmed their numbers into the speed dial, along with a host of others.

Andre leans out, smiles, and offers a hand to help me in. I'd love to slap that silly smirk right off his face.

"Lexi darling, what a surprise," he says with that slight Dutch accent I remember so well. The one that makes my soul soar.

This can't be an accident. I back away, indicate Steve and shake my head.

Hurt crosses his strong face fleetingly, but he gets my unspoken meaning. Not in front of Steve. One thing you have to give him, he's always quick on the uptake. He clears his face of any recognition.

"May I help you, Mrs. . . . ."

"Lexi Winslow."

"Please forgive my error. My friends call me Andre."

I want to say "You don't have any friends," but, come to think of it, I don't have any friends anymore, either. The few friends I did have started looking at me suspiciously when I was arrested. Then they disassociated themselves as rapidly as possible.

I wait, letting Steve get in the backseat ahead of me and sit in the middle, next to Andre. For once, I'm glad the kid's here.

"Hi. I'm Steve," Steve holds his hand out to Andre.

Steve falls back against his seat as the open jeep launches forward like it was shot from a canon.

I totally forgot. Drivers in Java, and apparently here in Sumatra, believe in driving as fast as possible. They must think they're racing because their only object is to overtake and pass any vehicle in front of them. The poor condition of the roads and head-on traffic don't faze them a bit. The mortality rate from auto crashes must be huge. Between the driving and Andre, my anxiety level shoots through the roof. Andre didn't really seem surprised to see me, but how could he possibly know I was coming? I didn't know myself until two days ago.

We soon leave civilization in our wake in a cloud of carbon soot. There are no vehicle pollution requirements here, either.

Our driver follows a winding dirt road through breathtaking hillsides terraced with rice fields and high waterfalls. Sumatra does have a paved road that rings the island, but the paved road is built where the ground is firm. That means it's inland from our hotel which is located on the coast and surrounded by dense jungle and large marshlands.

Later, we pass a sign saying "Kuljpm Unung National Park" and soon enter a dense, even more humid jungle. Above us, the overhead canopy of trees blocks out the sun. Around us, the jungle feels alive with birds calling and monkeys chattering in the trees. There's no shortage of bugs, either. I swat the umpteenth one in a row and brush it off my arm. Once, we even catch a glimpse of a large warthog with curled tusks.

I sense Andre studying my face as I force myself to stare fixedly at the passing landscape. I can't believe I'm sitting within two feet of him. It's not fair. It's like waving a box of See's dark chocolate butter creams in front of a diabetic. You know it will destroy you, but you can't resist having one—or two . . .

Steve taps the driver on his shoulder. "Ramelan, have you ever heard of boogey men?"

"Shh. Do not say name out loud."

Ramelan speeds up and his eyes scan the area fearfully.

"But they're not real, are they?" Steve asks.

"Most real. Most fierce. Steal children. Kill people."

Steve isn't sure if the driver is pulling his leg.

"They're Indonesian pirates who traverse the seas on their black-sailed prows. They sail on the monsoon winds. Raid, pillage, murder, cut whole families to little pieces."

"But this isn't the monsoon season," Steve says.

"Comes soon."

I smother a laugh.

Ramelan's conviction makes Steve glance around fearfully at the dark jungle.

I notice the corners of Andre's mouth go up in amusement.

I could tell Steve that Ramelan is historically accurate. Boogey men do still exist, but these days there are few of the gypsy pirates left. Most have moved on to a different form of piracy and become shipping traders.

Still it's fun to watch him worry. I'm worried, too, but my cause for concern already sits inside the jeep with us. My brain betrays me and recalls our time in Sydney. Riding the ferry out to swim at Bondi Beach, staying at the wineries in Brisbane, hiking through the Blue Mountains.

The jeep jerks to a full stop, snapping me back to the present. Andre smiles at me. It's almost like he was reading my mind. He points as twenty-seven feet of thick snake slithers slowly across the road in front of the jeep. Ramelan identifies it as a reticulated python.

Whatever kind of snake it is, it's the biggest I've ever seen. Not something anyone should grapple with in a one-on-one situation.

Speaking of snakes, what on earth is Andre doing here? His timing couldn't be worse. Can it really be a coincidence? His showing up in this out of the way place at this exact time? I don't believe it. This whole situation could spin out of control. The voice in my head is telling me to flee. I only wish I could.

With the snake gone, Ramelan drives on in the direction of the coast. As the hour gets later, the birds and the monkeys quiet and other, deeper, more predatory sounds emerge from the jungle making us all tense in the open jeep.

It's evening by the time we reach the Star of Sumatra Hotel on the coast. It's built with a nod to the Indonesian style of a Batak longhouse where the ends of the eaves curl upward like the prows of the native fishing boats. Its location on a low slope above a bay is perfection. Below and to the left, a river flows from the jungle through a marsh and into the calm bay. Boats dot the water. The place is a total surprise. I hadn't expected anything as beautiful and serene. I totally get why Karista Ochoa would want to come here. If it weren't for Denise's murder, I'd be positive she came for a vacation.

As our jeep pulls up to the entrance, we see red paper lanterns scattered up the drive. Their light makes for a welcoming glow.

CHAPTER 9

We enter the hotel, and step back in time to the colonial days when the British controlled Indonesia.

While the exterior of the hotel is enchanting, the interior holds problems for me. The twenty or so cages hanging around the room and filled with beautiful exotic birds are freaking me out. I know that songbirds are highly prized in this country, but I have a serious thing about birds in cages. Or any wild animal in a cage, but particularly birds. Birds should be up in the sky, flying free.

Then there's a wall completely covered with a display of knives. My stomach churns. A whole wall of them. Aside from the fact that I loathe them, all those sharp points must be extremely bad feng shui. The gods must be very unhappy with this place.

Technically, they're antique knives and swords of

delicate Indonesian metal work—cutlasses and curved ornamental bronze daggers . . . curved daggers? That rings a bell with me. I just can't remember why. Seeing Andre has rattled my brain. I'll have to think about it later.

I don't know which I dislike more, the birds or the knives. I'm going to have to avoid this room.

The attractive, young Indian woman behind the registration desk says, "My name is Ifrah. How may I help you?" Her smile is beamed at Steve. I admit he's an attractive boy. He did well in the gene pool lottery. He looks like his mother's family and not his father's.

"Reservations for two in the names of Winslow and Winslow," Steve says. The clerk pulls up our reservation on the computer system. Andre's standing right behind us. I can feel his breath on the back of my neck. I wish Ifrah would work faster. I want a door between Andre and me as soon as possible.

"Here it is," she reads. "Our best suite, Mr. and Mrs. Winslow."

Steve starts to protest. I cut him off.

"We'll need two rooms please. This is my nephew," I tell her.

Ifrah shakes her head. "Please accept my apologies. Your reservation was made only yesterday and I explained to Mr. Howard Sutton that the suite was the only room available. He assured me that the suite would be fine. There is a sofa bed in the living room."

"The suite will be nice," I say.

Andre is so close behind me that I hear the sharp intake of his breath.

#

The bellboy leads us into the suite. It's an airy, colonial-style room like the lobby, but without the caged birds and the sharp metalwork. Ceiling fans rotate slowly. There's a large living room. On a table, sits an ice bucket with a bottle of champagne and two crystal flutes. To one side is a spacious bedroom with a kingsize bed. The large bathroom has a deep, old-fashioned clawfoot bathtub. Outside, a wide veranda runs the entire length of the building with all the rooms opening onto it.

The suite's walls are white, and the floors are dark mahogany. The bamboo chairs are covered with colorful Malaysian batik prints, and there are touches of Sumatran woodcarving and brass art scattered about. Thankfully there are no knives.

The bellboy lets us know dinner will be served in an hour at the restaurant. In response to my question, he confirms there is room service and leaves.

I throw open the doors onto the veranda and step outside. The tropical evening engulfs me, and I find myself overlooking the bay.

A small, green-crested Sumatran lizard skitters along the railing. Lizards are a good thing here. They keep the bugs down.

Out on the water, I can see outrigger fishing boats with

painted magical eyes eerily visible on their high prows. They're heading for the open water of the Strait of Malacca and the night's fishing. Slightly out of character is the large, modern, ocean-going yacht anchored in the center of the bay. Yet somehow, at this moment, the blend of exotic and modern feels natural.

Even the soft, melodic drum and flute music drifting from somewhere in the distance is magical. I inhale deeply. In any other circumstances, I would love it here.

Inside, Steve's finishing his call to Howard about his stolen documents. He calls out to me. "Anything you want to add before I hang up?"

"Make sure he gets you on Interpol's Stolen and Lost Document List."

He does and hangs up. Minutes later, he joins me with two glasses of champagne. I take one.

"Did I have to be a nephew? You know that makes me look like your boy toy, right?"

"Actually that's a pretty good idea for a cover story. Men get to travel with "nieces." Why shouldn't women get to travel with "nephews"." You'll look fine. I'll look like a cradle robber. We say you're my relative, but we'll act like lovers. I like it. It's a good cover." And it will back Andre off, I tell myself.

"I'm no kid. I'm twenty-four."

"Exactly."

He starts to bristle. "Do I get boyfriend privileges?"

"Pretend is the operative word."

He sips his drink. "Okay." He pauses. "You know, I could get used to this. So what do we do next, honey?"

I tune him out.

He taps my arm to get my attention. "Seriously? What next?"

"We can discuss the situation at breakfast. For now, I'm going to have dinner in my room, take a long hot bath in that beautiful tub, and follow it with a good night's sleep in the bed. I suggest you do the same, but on the living room couch."

"Wouldn't you like to take that hot bath with your nephew?"

Not in this lifetime.

#

It must be around one in the morning. The bedroom is dark except for the pools of moonlight through the veranda doors.

The door lock clicks open and Andre steps in. He pulls the curtains closed. I'd forgotten how well he moves, light on his feet and balanced like an athlete. I guess constant running from the authorities will do that for you.

I flip on the light beside the bed. I'm fully dressed and waiting. Andre isn't surprised. "Finally, Monsieur Van der Meer. I expected you earlier."

"Ms. Winslow. Is that any way to greet an old friend?" He seats himself on the side of the bed.

"Is that what we are? Friends?"

"That's not by my choice. I see you're still wearing the necklace."

My hand flies to my silver cross. I'd totally forgotten I had it on. I tuck it inside my blouse.

I twist out of his reach as he moves closer. "A call over the past two years would have been nice," I say.

"If the police were monitoring your calls, it would have looked bad for you. I didn't want to add to your problems."

"It was terrible," I blurt out, my pain evident. I wish I could take it back before the last word is out.

"I'm so sorry."

He tries to put his arms around me, but I push him away.

"You're angry with me?"

I struggle to get my emotions under control. "That surprises you?"

"But you know business has to come before pleasure."

My chest tightens. "Of course it does."

He takes my hand. His touch makes my skin tingle. I snatch it back. I could lose control of this situation in a heartbeat.

"Are you armed?" I ask in an effort to distract him.

He nods.

"Do you have a spare?"

He reaches behind his back and hands me a Glock 17. "Take this one. It's just like yours."

How does he know that? I wonder. But I resist asking.

I notice he's wearing a shoulder holster with a second gun. Two guns? Andre rarely carries one. Something must have him worried.

"Are you expecting trouble?"

"This isn't a safe place."

"Then why are you here?" I ask.

"Van der Meer happens to be my favorite name, but it's become known to several people I'd rather it hadn't. I need a new one." He looks at me warmly. "It conjures up many fond memories, but personal safety must come first."

"If it's fake documents you want, there's a French woman and a beggar at the airport I can introduce you to."

"Too late. I've already made my arrangements."

Here? It would be nice if Andre could tell the truth for a few minutes, or is he telling the truth? I never know with him.

He leans toward me. "I've missed you."

I lift the Glock before he can embrace me.

"You would shoot me with my own gun?"

I nod.

"Why? Because of that wet behind the ears pup next door? And don't insult me by saying he's your nephew. You don't have a nephew."

"What do you care?"

"I don't like the way he follows your every move."

"You stay away from him. He's a nice boy."

"This is what you've come to? Picking up an adolescent like that?"

"You're jealous," I say in surprise. "As I recall, paintings are more important to you than relationships."

He smiles. "You mean the portrait of the Countess Orsini's ancestral Grandmother? She certainly was not an attractive woman. I wonder whatever possessed an artist like Rembrandt to paint her."

"He probably needed the money."

"I can relate to that."

"I should turn you over to the authorities right now."

He's surprised. "Anger doesn't become you."

"Being abandoned has that effect on me."

Andre's such a good actor. He genuinely seems concerned. It's infuriating.

"You sound like you don't trust me."

"Do I really need to answer that?"

"Fair enough. I'm not perfect, you know. But you can't question my feelings for you."

He moves closer to me—daring me to shoot. The Glock wavers, and then I lower it. He knows me too well.

He takes me into his arms and kisses me tenderly. My head swims as my body responds. In one moment, he's released every feeling for him that I've tried to kill.

No. This can't happen. I force myself to raise the gun. "You should leave."

"Must I? As you please. Until tomorrow. Dream of me, Cherie."

Really? The man could charm snakes. Even worse, I probably will dream of him tonight. He makes me livid.

What makes him think he can just waltz in here like nothing ever happened? Is that it? Is it nothing to him?

And how does he know I use a Glock? I've only recently bought one?

I call out to him as he slips out the veranda door. "There won't be a next time."

Silence.

My hands are shaking violently. They're doing that way too much lately. I have to find a way to make them stop.

I put the Glock down quickly on the bedside table so I don't shoot myself.

I glance across the room. The door to the living room is slowly closing. How long has Steve been behind it, listening?

Furious, I stride over and yank it open.

I catch him totally off guard as his hand on the doorknob drags him into the bedroom. He sprawls at my feet.

"Don't you ever eavesdrop on me again." He stands and tries to bluster his way out of it. "Who is that guy?"

"Someone you should stay away from."

"You two act pretty chummy."

"Go to bed."

"Will you tuck me in?"

I push him into the living room and slam the door behind him.

As I turn, a flutter in the curtains at the veranda door

catches my eye. I rush toward it.

"Andre, this is too much?"

No one's there. It must have been a trick of the wind.

I climb back into bed and reach for the Glock. I go to slip it under the pillow, but as I do, my fingers touch something else. Something metallic. I lift the pillow to find a handful of bullets underneath.

What? I quickly check the gun. The magazine is empty. No wonder he felt safe with me aiming the gun at him. I should have known. Andre's a man who takes self preservation very seriously.

CHAPTER 10

Breakfast takes place on a lovely patio surrounded by dark pink bougainvillea and overlooking the water. Several of the caged birds are singing. Their beautiful voices are a treat to hear, until I remember they're in cages.

I identify with them. At the moment, I feel trapped having to be here, so close to Andre.

Below, a dinghy from the yacht is tied up to a long dock. The dock needs to be a long one, because now that it's daylight, I can see that a marsh lies between the hotel and the bay. The dock's walkway goes above the swampy areas, connecting the hotel to the water.

I sip my coffee and munch on a croissant while surveying the guests at the other tables. My sunglasses cover the dark rings around my eyes. I tossed and turned all last night after Andre left. He was right. I did dream about him. I wish there was an operation to have people permanently removed from your mind. If there was, I'd be first in line.

There's no sign of Karista or Javier yet. I do see an elderly man with a cane who carries himself with old world dignity and eats alone. He looks like he might be Spanish or Portuguese. At the farthest table, sits a sturdy, middle-aged couple, who appear to be British. The woman has on a church-type flowered hat and the man wears Bermuda shorts with knee socks. Stereotypical of me to think they're British, but it's hard not to. She's busy writing a stack of postcards. He's smoking a pipe.

There are several younger couples of mixed ages and nationalities, and one American couple with two young boys. The boys are currently engaged in a food fight, which their parents are ineffectively trying to stop. One piece of mango narrowly misses a waiter, but only because he manages to duck in time.

No such luck for me. The next piece of flying debris, a marmalade-covered scone, lands in my lap. I wave off the apologies of the couple and accept a wetted napkin from the stoic waiter. It's bad enough that I dribble food on my clothes myself, but I seriously resent the contributions of others.

All-in-all, there's an interesting mix of people out here in the middle of the jungle. There's no sign of Andre this morning. I don't know which is worse, him hanging around or having to wonder what he's up to.

Steve slides into the chair across from me. He's

wearing a bright neon green batik shirt. I'm glad I have my sunglasses on or I might be blinded.

The waiter fills his cup, tops off mine, and leaves.

"Where did you get that shirt?" I have to ask.

"Isn't it great? The hotel shop has a great selection."

"I wouldn't call it inconspicuous."

"I bought three of them. Remember, I have no clothes."

Behind him, I notice a striking man who I'd guess to be Portuguese and in his mid forties feeding the birds. A magnificent parrot rides on his shoulder. The man's crisp, white shirt is open to the waist, revealing a well-developed chest. All he needs is a cutlass and a headband, and he could star in any pirate movie. Move over Fabio, this man could grace the cover of any romance novel.

"I wonder who the bird keeper is."

Steve gives the man a dismissive glance. "So what's next?"

"We act like tourists and watch for Karista and Javier."

I try to stop my eyes from darting back to the man with the parrot.

The waiter offers a tray of fruit to Steve. He reaches for a banana with his left hand, pausing when he sees my warning look, remembers what I told him, and switches to his right hand. The correct one for eating in most of the world.

"Thank you. We're fine for now."

The waiter departs.

"Shouldn't we be out casing the place? Find out where Karista and Javier are?"

"We're surrounded on three sides by jungle and one by water. This is the only restaurant for miles. If they eat, they'll show up soon."

As if on cue, Karista and Javier step out on the patio. They receive instant deference from the staff as another waiter escorts them to the table with the best view.

Karista wears a pretty designer sundress with a yellow floral pattern that fits her slim body perfectly. She's topped the outfit with the big floppy yellow hat Sherry mentioned and a happy smile. Javier has on linen slacks, a short sleeved cotton shirt, and his plantation hat. Both have on large, dark sunglasses and nice suntans. They look every inch a beautiful, wealthy couple on vacation.

I pull my cell phone out. I can't make a call from this remote area but I can grab a photo of him. But with the sunglasses and the hat he's wearing, there's no way I can get a useful shot. I wonder if they wear those sunglasses and hats 24-7? Like in the shower or to bed or while having sex?

Javier looks different in person than I expected from the grainy airport videos. He has a strong, chiseled face with a stocky build and powerful muscles. Over all, he's much tougher physically than I anticipated. He looks like he plays a competitive sport Soccer maybe? He has that kind of athletic body.

Javier waves the breakfast host away and pulls out

Karista's chair for her. Quite the polite young man, just like Steve, I think. Once seated, the waiters hover around them. Coffee, juice, fruit, and pastries appear instantly. Karista and Javier talk intimately while the waiters do their thing. Interesting. They're definitely getting what I would call the royal treatment.

I look at Steve. "Sure doesn't look like a kidnapping to me."

His disappointment is evident. "How do we find out if they killed Denise?"

Good question. And one I can't answer. I have no idea. I guess I could walk up and ask them, but I doubt they'll tell me.

"You want to call your father and let him know Karista is all right?"

"Not on your life. He'll yell at me about being robbed at the airport. "

Steve splits after breakfast. As I'm leaving, I pause near the low stone wall surrounding the patio to enjoy the attractive scene of the bay below. Maybe I'll go down later for a swim.

The elderly man with a cane stops beside me. "I hope you're enjoying your stay."

"Yes, it's a lovely place."

"You see that large yacht in the center? It belongs to my son."

He points proudly to the large ocean-going yacht.

"She's an elegant ship. It must be beautiful inside." I

respond.

"Would you like to see it? I could arrange it with him."

"I'd love that, but I'm sure it would be too much trouble."

"Please allow me to introduce myself. I'm Alfonso Luis de Alevado."

"Lexi Winslow."

"I'll check if it's possible and let you know. Her name is The Star of Sumatra."

"The same name as the hotel?"

Alfonso nods. "The hotel also belongs to my son. The Star of Java was the name of our family's palm oil plantation."

"Then your son is very successful. You must be proud. I've never been to a real plantation. Is it nearby?"

"We no longer have possession of it. There were bad times."

"I'm sorry."

He nods again and moves away.

I do know the palm oil is Sumatra's biggest export. Sadly, the slash and burn technique used to create land for the palms has decimated the Sumatran jungles and wildlife. Always a hard choice between feeding your family and saving the environment.

Back upstairs in our suite, I retrieve the sat phone from my carry-on bag and take it out to the veranda. I dial not caring about the time difference in Beverly Hills. Morgan answers immediately.

"Lexi? It's about time. What do you think you're doing encouraging Steve to go with you? I want him put on the next plane home."

I tune him out. Poor Steve. I never thought about how miserable it must be living with Morgan as his father. I'm amazed that Steve is as nice as he is. I know he doesn't get it from his mother. She's a social climber of the worst sort.

Morgan finally winds down.

I let silence be my answer.

"Lexi, are you there?"

Ah. It must be my turn to speak. "We saw Karista and Javier. It's definitely not looking like a kidnapping. Let Kevin know that they appear to be having a good time with no sign of coercion."

"I knew it was a fool's errand. I'll tell Kevin."

"What's going on with the search for Karista's and Denise's social media sites?"

"It's bogged down. Police are trying to get a search warrant for the host's cached files. They're not exactly being helpful. I'll expect you both on the next plane to Los Angeles. You can be back to work by the end of the week."

"Morgan, we just got here. That's what the situation looks like on the surface. Give me a couple more days to be sure and then we'll be back."

Now there's a pause from his end.

Finally he says, "I guess Steve can stay, too, since it doesn't sound like there's any threat."

"What's happening about Denise?" I ask.

"Autopsy confirms she was killed with a weird serpentine knife --"

An alarm rings in my head. That's where I heard 'curved knife.'

"-- about the time Karista and Javier left. The police are hot to talk to them."

How stupid am I? Of course, the curved knife.

"Morgan, did they find the knife?"

"Not that I heard."

"This hotel has a lobby wall entirely decorated with antique serpentine knives and swords."

"Seriously? That's not good. You're positive Karista's okay? I don't want anything happen to her."

"Look, I'm going to talk with Karista and see if I get a sense if they're involved in Denise's death."

"I don't know. Kevin won't like it if he finds out you're there asking questions about the murder on his money."

"Have they cleared Sherry?"

"They haven't arrested her yet, but they're seriously thinking about it. Kevin's lawyer forced them to back off, although it may only be temporary."

"I can't believe she's involved. Surely she has no motive."

"Maybe the police know something we don't."

"True. They're not interested in motive, just means and opportunity."

"One other thing. All her credit cards and ID are missing. Someone ran up some big charges here locally the day after she died. The police are looking for any surveillance videos."

"That makes it unlikely that the murderer is Karista or Javier."

"Lexi, if the police show up there and try to arrest Karista, Kevin wants you to whisk her out of there."

"That might be easier said than done, Morgan."

I'm not intervening with the police or mounting a jailbreak. Especially not if she's guilty. But that looks unlikely since Karista and Javier were gone the same day as Denise's murder. I guess the cards and ID could have been passed off to someone. I try to change the subject. "Any luck identifying Javier?"

"No photographs of Javier have turned up and Sherry's sketch makes him look like a demented killer on steroids. No fingerprints, either, after all the time he spent in that house."

"Sherry said he acted like a hypochondriac, always using antiseptic wipes. Pretty smart cover for not leaving fingerprints." I give him a description of Javier and add, "I'm going to pick up a camera in the gift shop and grab a picture of him. I'll send it this afternoon."

There's another long pause on Morgan's end of the line. Then he says, "I expect you to watch out for Steve."

I bite back what I'd really like to say and instead reply, "Steve's fine. Please thank Howard for the suite. We're so enjoying it."

"You're in a suite with my son?"

He's still squawking as I hang up the phone.

Paybacks are such fun. But, the use of a curved knife in Denise's murder and the curved knives on the wall here? Not amusing.

Karista was in Indonesia before with Kevin. Could she have purchased one as a souvenir? Has Javier ever been to Indonesia before? We need to find out who he really is.

It's interesting that Sherry mentioned he used antiseptic wipes. There wasn't any sign of a bacteria phobia this morning. There are too many unanswered questions. I think I'll cruise their suite and see what I can find. Only first, I'll need to find what room they're in.

I retrieve a silk scarf from my suitcase and head for the lobby.

CHAPTER 11

I force myself to walk through the lobby. Between the birds and the pointy knives, I need a pair of horse blinders just to get to the reception desk. Steve is there, chatting with Ifrah. Nothing wrong with his taste in women. Ifrah seems like a nice person.

As I approach, she's warning him not to go near the mangroves at the mouth of the river or the bay alone. "There are crocodiles," she says.

I forgot there would be salt water crocodiles around. I've heard about them. Those are the ones that grow well over twenty feet and weigh up to four thousand pounds. They have no trouble swimming the ocean between Indonesia and Australia, or even in fresh water. Not to mention they're known man-eaters. I silently thank her for the warning. Nothing could tempt me to go near the bay now. I'll do my swimming this afternoon at the pool.

I catch Ifrah's attention by waving my scarf. "Excuse me. The young lady in the yellow sundress and hat dropped this on the patio after breakfast. Do you know who I mean?"

She nods.

"Could you please return it for me?"

I can feel Steve studying me. Ifrah reaches for the scarf. "Of course, mademoiselle. I'll be happy to put it in her box. She carefully folds it and places it into an open letter box on the wall behind her for the guest rooms. The scarf goes into the one marked 314.

It's an old trick, but, like now, it frequently works.

I can tell Steve immediately gets what I'm doing. Good. At least he's observant. I wander toward the stairway and pause idly at a table covered with magazines and newspapers. I spot Andre by the stairs talking with the bird man from the patio. I smile. Those are two attractive men. Their intense discussion makes me wonder how well they know each other.

I pick up a magazine from the table and head out to the patio to kill some time. Now that breakfast is over, Karista and Javier may be back in their rooms. I sit at a table an order a cappuccino to kill time.

The patio is deserted except for one woman finishing her food. She's in her late thirties with a sweet, charming face and the kind of natural figure that a trophy wife would kill for. She's wearing a ring on her left hand with a sapphire the size of the rock of Gibraltar.

Andre enters. Uh, oh. He's headed my way. As he passes the woman's table, she puts out a hand to stop him. They exchange a few words and he sits down with her. The conversation appears quite engaging. I wonder who she is. A friend of his maybe? Is she here to meet him?

Uh, oh. His mouth just went straight and tight. I know that look. He only does that when he's really serious about something.

Listen to me. Here I am, worrying about Andre talking with another woman. What does that say about me? Am I jealous? How can I be? I loathe him, right? Am I a total loser? Crooks are my business. Why can't I see what Andre is?

The cappuccino I ordered arrives and so does Steve. His glance at Andre is not friendly. His eyes shift to take in the woman sitting next to him. The sight of her makes him smile with pleasure. Men. Finally, he turns to me.

"You got Karista's room number. What are you planning?"

"Lower your voice and order something."

"I just ate. And so did you. Why are we here?"

"We're not doing anything."

"I'm your partner."

My cutting laugh makes him turn red.

"You can't shut me out."

I just smile.

"I . . . I'll—"

"What? Tell daddy?"

I give him credit for control. I couldn't have struck a nerve any better than if I'd used a dental drill. He stands slowly, managing not to say anything and stalks away.

Okay. That was mean of me. Still, it's better he's not involved in case things go sour. After finishing my cappuccino, I stroll around the hotel. By now, Karista and Javier should be settled in somewhere for the morning. I just have to locate them.

I start in the spa. A glance at the schedule shows neither of their names. They're not shopping in the hotel store, so I buy a digital camera and a USB cable for it. A chat with the concierge confirms Karista and Javier are not on today's photo safari trip into the jungle or to one of the recently discovered ruins. That leaves the pool.

And there they are, oiling each other's backs affectionately. With books and a pitcher of sangria on the table next to them, they look settled in for a while. Perfect.

Minutes later, I'm at the third floor stairway door and peering down the hallway. Just my luck, two maids are chatting at the far end of the hall, right in front of room three-one-four.

I notice that there are only six rooms on this floor, unlike the eight rooms on our floor below. Must be because this it the top floor and the roof narrows above it.

Ten minutes later, the maids are still talking.

Even worse luck, I hear someone hurrying up the stairwell at my back. I have to choose quickly. Either I step into the third floor hall where the maids can see me, or I turn and walk down the stairwell like any other hotel guest. Not much of a choice. I head downstairs.

I miss a step when Javier's head, and then the rest of him, come into view. He's moving lightly, like a cat. If it weren't for the maids, I'd have opened the old-fashioned lock to their room easily by sliding a credit card through the jamb and he'd have caught me inside. I manage to nod politely as I pass him. Behind me, his footsteps pause. I can feel his eyes studying my back.

My legs are wobbly by the time I reach the lobby and my heart is beating faster than it should. That was way too close a call.

I manage to ignore the knives and the birds and grab a newspaper off a table. Collapsing onto a sofa, I pretend to read. I try to get control of my nerves. As near misses go, that was a definite squeaker.

I don't even know if he's guilty of Denise's murder. But up close, Javier made every hair on my body stand up. How can that be? It's an odd reaction to an otherwise nice young man. I can't find any reason to explain it other than I must be way more tired than I thought after all those hours on planes. I can't sleep on flights, and last night, all I did was toss and turn.

Andre sits down beside me. "Are you okay?"

"Of course," I lie. "Why do you ask?"

He turns my newspaper right-side-up and indicates the page I'm looking at. "Do you have a sudden unbridled desire to buy an ox?"

I realize I'm holding the Sumatran equivalent of the classified section.

Andre looks at me quizzically. Okay. Now I feel like a total idiot. I thought the up-side-down newspaper bit only happened in bad movies. I must be way more exhausted than I think.

He takes my hands in his and rubs them lightly. I can feel myself relaxing. I snatch them back quickly. "Stop that," I say.

"Care to tell me about it?"

"No."

He nods and sits back. "You're really tense. Come up to my room. I can give you a relaxing back rub."

"That's not going to happen."

"We need to have a serious talk. In private where we won't be disturbed." he says.

"I think your actions have spoken clearly enough."

Javier exits the stairwell and heads back toward the pool. Andre notices me tense as I watch him.

"Has that man done something to you?"

"No, of course not. I don't even know him." Even as I talk, I can tell how lame I sound.

"Did you talk with Grace?" he asks. From my blank expression he adds, "The woman who spoke to me at breakfast. You might find her story interesting."

Before I can ask why, Andre spots Steve heading toward us. "Not again. Have you really turned into one of those cat women who likes little boys?"

Is he deliberately trying to make me mad? "That's a cougar, not a cat. And Steve is hardly little."

Andre gives me a look. I can't deny any relationship with Steve or I'll lose our cover story for being here. Still, I can feel the heat on my face as I blush. Does he really believe I'm old enough to be a cougar?

"I'm serious, Andre. Leave him alone."

"We'll see." He pecks me quickly on the cheek before I can stop him.

"Until later." He leaves as Steve arrives.

"I don't like that guy," mutters Steve.

"Then you're even. He doesn't like you, either." I stand to go.

Steve blurts out, "Why did my father hire you when you have a criminal record?"

That stops me. "How'd you find that out?"

He smiles. "I tricked your file out of Gail in HR.

"Then you know I was cleared."

"No. You were let go for lack of evidence. I looked it up on the Internet. That's a big difference."

Really, the boy is too nosy for his own good.

"Ask Andre," I say over my shoulder as I head for our room to change for the pool.

CHAPTER 12

As I'm slipping into my bikini, I hear Steve stomp into the living room.

Seconds later, there's a knock on our door to the suite. I pull on my cover-up and go to answer it. Steve heads for the door at the same time.

"You expecting someone?" he says.

I shake my head. The knock comes again.

"Wait."

Ducking back in my room, I remove Andre's gun from my bag on the bed and return. Steve's eyes widen at the sight of the Glock.

A key rattles in the lock.

I slide behind the door and motion Steve to the other side.

The doorknob turns.

I hold my breath as it slowly opens.

It's the bellboy. He enters carrying a vase with an enormous arrangement of branches of delicate violet orchids. They look like tiny butterflies.

"Hello? Anyone here?" he calls.

I slip the gun into my cover-up's pocket.

Steve steps in front of him. Startled, the bellboy drops the vase.

Steve grabs it before it hits the floor. The bellboy snatches the vase back and moves the beautiful floral arrangement to a nearby table. "So sorry. For the lady."

I step from behind the door. "Thank you."

Good thing he'd put the flowers down or they would definitely have hit the ground this time.

"Many pardons. No one answered my knock."

Steve tips him, and he can't leave fast enough.

"Where did you get that gun?" Steve demands. "Why do you even need one?"

I ignore him and walk out on the veranda where I stare out to sea, lost in thought. It's going to take more than flowers, Andre. Don't you ever take no for an answer?

Steve picks a small envelope out of the flowers and opens it. He looks surprised by what he reads. He hands it to me. "They're from some guy named Vito Leon de Alevado. With an invitation for us to dine on his ship tonight. Who's Vito?"

I shake my head, then remember. The old man I talked to on the patio earlier about the ship was named Alfonso de Alevado. Vito must be his son.

"The son of a man I met this morning."

"What does he want?"

"Dinner apparently."

#

Ditching Steve, I head for the pool. The majority of the guests are there, including the two little boys, the pretty woman I saw after breakfast on the patio, and the British couple, who are both bright pink and risking serious sunburn.

Javier and Karista are still there, too. And he has his sunglasses and hat off. It's the perfect time to grab a photo.

I can feel Javier's eyes following me as I spread towels on a lounge chair. Then I take the new camera from my bag and take pictures of the bay, the pool, the hotel, and the gardens like any overzealous tourist would.

I even photograph a small monitor lizard. There are several hanging about. I hope never to meet their largest relatives, the komodo dragons. They're native to Indonesia, too, but their home is the area around Komodo Island, which is farther east.

But I can't get a good direct shot of Karista and Javier without it being obvious.

Suddenly the twin boys from breakfast are jumping up and down in front of me. "Take our picture, take our picture." Their mother rushes over. "Turner, Taylor. Stop bothering the lady."

It's a small thing to do, so I offer to take pictures of the three of them. They smile and pose. Suddenly I realize that Karista and Javier are directly behind them. How perfect. I happily click pictures. Dozens of them. I even use the zoom a couple times. I ask the mother for her email and promise to send the pictures when I get home. Minus the ones of Javier, of course.

That done, I replace the camera in my bag. It slips down next to my . . . Andre's Glock. I forgot I'd left it in my bag.

I jump in the pool and swim for a while. It feels good to stretch after all the hours of sitting motionless in planes. Finally relaxed, I float on my back, enjoying the beautiful blue sky. Sadly, those troubling questions keep circling my brain and won't go away. In spite of what Morgan said, should I tell Karista about Denise? Or was she involved and already knows? Would I be exposing Steve and me?

I still need answers. The only place I might find them is in their room. I'll have to try again. Not something I'm looking forward to.

My thoughts are interrupted when water splashes up my nose. Kids, I think as I blow out the water. My eyes clear. It's not the kids, it's the woman with the big sapphire ring swimming toward me. The one who stopped Andre this morning.

"Hi, I'm Grace," she says with a southern accent. "Isn't this a great place?"

Small talk. Not something I'm good at. I give her my first name and agree it is a nice place. I wonder what

Andre wanted me to hear.

"My Walt couldn't get away. That's my fiancé. He didn't want me to come alone, but I couldn't wait any longer." She adds. "Did you see that good-lookin' man at breakfast? He was just scrumptious. And nice, too."

She must mean Andre. "No, I didn't notice," I reply. So much for her engagement.

"He had on the light blue linen shirt."

Yep, that's Andre. I shake my head. "Sorry."

"That's a nice lookin' young man you're with. I see why you don't notice other guys."

Someone please save me. Is this woman on the prowl or what? She'd be perfectly at home in Beverly Hills. Someone should warn poor Walt. I don't respond to Grace, but she doesn't notice.

"Have you been here long?" she continues.

"Since last night."

"Shoot, I was hopin' to meet someone who might have met my sister, Emmy Lou Tyler, when she was here. I've been askin' all the guests."

That seems odd, but I suggest, "Have you tried the staff?"

"I did. No one remembers her, and she's not even in their records."

"Grace..?"

She pauses.

"Why don't you just ask your sister whatever you need to know? Is she missing?"

"She disappeared six months ago. This is the last place I know she visited."

"You're positive it was here?"

"Yes. I got a postcard from her. She specifically mentioned this hotel."

Uh oh. I don't like the sound of that. "Grace, your fiancé might have been right. Sometimes it's not good to travel alone."

"She's my sister. I have to find her."

"Why don't you join my nephew and me for breakfast tomorrow?"

"Oh, he's your nephew?" I can see she doesn't believe me. "I'd love to join you."

I lie back, floating again as she heads off. My thoughts aren't good. The biggest of which is how Andre knew I'd be interested in Grace's story?

CHAPTER 13

Around eight, there's a knock on the door to our suite. I open it and find myself face-to-face with the handsome man I'd seen this morning with the parrot.

"Ms Winslow? Good evening. I'm Vito Leon de Alevado."

So the old man's son is the handsome bird man that owns the hotel. Interesting. Behind him is a tough looking man who looks like he can lift weights with his teeth.

"This is Sajuk, my assistant."

From Sajuk's muscular physical appearance, he's most likely a bodyguard, but I nod politely in his direction.

"This is my nephew, Steve. Your father was kind to pass along my admiration of your impressive yacht."

"I'm glad he did. He knows I enjoy showing it off to our guests."

Vito graciously helps me step out of the dinghy and onto the lowered swimming platform of the Star of Sumatra. Steve follows. Sajuk secures the dinghy and vanishes into the ship.

"I didn't see any crocodiles around the dock," Steve comments.

I didn't, either, and I was definitely looking for them.

"Our employees chase them away," Vito says. "Losing guests could ruin our reputation."

I wouldn't like to be the employee with that job. Sounds like Vito's more concerned with the loss of reputation than the loss of guests or employees. I read recently that in Darwin, Australia, people are actually paying to be submerged in the equivalent of a shark cage while chum is fed to circling crocodiles weighing over a ton.

Darwin? I wonder if that's where the Darwin Awards began. The one for stupid people who should be weeded out in the survival of the fittest.

I look around as Vito leads us through the passageways and gives us a tour. "Your ship is beautiful," I manage to say and truly mean.

"It's from Royal Seas Line."

Steve's also doing a nice job of pretending to be affectionate by patting my arm and holding my hand.

"On the open sea, the ship has a thirty-five knot sprint speed."

Vito leads us up to the master bedroom on the upper deck. The suite, the view, and the decor are fabulous. Clean, sleek, and contemporary. Brushed stainless steel and aluminum with leather seating and wall coverings. I love function over form and this ship is all about function.

But what I'm blown away by most is the small drawing over the bed. I'm fairly good on the subject of European and American art. Many of the bank's customers buy art, and we get involved in the financing, insurance, and transferring of funds. Unless I'm totally crazy, that drawing of a bull fight is by the great Spanish artist, Francisco José de Goya y Lucientes. Goya for short.

Is that why Andre is really here? Sucking up to Vito to get access to the drawing? He does have a penchant for art by the masters. If he's really waiting for fake documents as he says, why pick a hotel out here in the boonies? A hotel in the city makes more sense to wait for a delivery. Screw him. If he steals this painting while I'm here, I can kiss my career goodbye.

Odd that Vito hasn't mentioned the drawing to us. Most owners love to brag about their art.

"Lexi, did you hear me?" Steve says.

I come back to the present and notice Vito looking at me oddly. "Sorry. I was overwhelmed by how lovely your yacht is. Is that a real Goya?"

Vito glances at it before saying, "Only a first-rate copy."

And if that's true, I have a bridge in Brooklyn I'd like

to sell him.

He turns abruptly and heads down the stairs. We follow.

How strange. Why would he lie? That drawing is an original. I'd bet my life on it. Maybe it's a security thing, and he doesn't want people to know.

Dinner is served on the fantail. The view of the shoreline is wonderful. Steve listens avidly as Vito continues on and on about his yacht.

"The Star has sleeping for eight guests and a crew of eight."

An elderly Sumatran man serves us appetizers of traditional smooth and steamy hors d'oeuvres wrapped in leaves with hot tea to drink. We help ourselves using our fingers. I love Asian food. It comes mostly in bite-size and doesn't require a knife.

I'm about to slap Steve, though. He's decided to hand feed me as part of our lovey-dovey relationship charade. One more "Here, dear, try this" and having food thrust at me and I won't be able to stop myself.

It occurs to me that the waiter is the only crew person I've seen.

"Where is your crew now?"

"Since we're at home, all but a skeleton crew are on leave."

Steve asks, "I saw you earlier today with a large parrot. It's a magnificent bird."

"Yes, that would be Cecilia. She lives in my office.

Birds are my treasures."

More like your prisoners, I think.

"Cecilia is sixty-eight."

"Where did she come from?" I say.

"She was a gift from my grandfather."

I wait for him to continue, but he doesn't. Instead, he changes the subject.

"So what brings you and your nephew so far from home?"

"I needed a vacation and decided to get as far from the rat race as possible. Steve agreed to keep me company."

"Most people who visit are amused at my country's backward culture and our prehistoric jungle tribes. Then they return to their superior rat race, laughing at us." This guy has a bit of a chip on his shoulder.

"Surely you have the last laugh at their failure to appreciate the unspoiled beauty and the serenity found here. There's true elegance in Indonesia's culture."

"You are one of the few who sees beyond the surface." The waiter replaces the hors d'oeuvres with soft and crunchy rice dishes accompanied by fish with a curry sauce.

Steve holds a bit of the fish in front of my mouth. "Here dear, open up." I manage not to choke on it. I even smile back at him while batting my eyelids as I kick his knee hard under the table. It's a pleasure to watch him try to hide the pain.

I turn to Vito. "You flatter me. Have you been in

Sumatra long?"

"My great grandfather came with his bride from Lisbon to take control of a palm oil plantation in eighteen ninety-one. Eventually, he bought it from the owners."

"What an adventure that must have been," Steve says.

"Sadly not a profitable one. His grandson, my father, made foolish mistakes and lost the plantation to unscrupulous government tax agents."

"How awful. What did he do?" I say.

"Like all displaced persons, he begged, and he starved."

Poor Alfonso. No empathy from his son. No love, either.

Steve's at a loss on how to respond. I try to help him out.

"There was no family in Portugal who could help?"

"De Alevados do not beg. What did relatives care of poor relations living far away? Especially when we were disowned by the rest of the family."

No love, indeed. "There must be a happy ending. Now you have this lovely hotel and ship."

"This was originally the location of my great-grandfather's vacation house. It's the first portion of his estate I've managed to buy back. The British corporation that has our plantation refuses to sell, unless we pay an exorbitant sum of money."

I say, "I'm sorry to hear that." While I can't help thinking that the sale price of a real Goya would more than pay for any plantation. What's with that?

Vito continues, "That will change soon. They're already having a hard time hiring workers. Another few months, and I'll take control."

Sounds like there's some sabotage going on at the plantation with Vito as the instigator. I note that even his eyes have changed. They're fierce and calculating, like a jungle cat speculating what his prey will taste like when he crunches down on its bones. I think Vito could be a very dangerous man to cross. I can see Steve considering his words, too.

"That's impressive, Vito," I say. "To rise from such a loss and develop all this."

He relaxes. "I will let nothing stop me until I recover all the property."

I believe him. I can recognize a fanatic when I see one. Two men in one day that give me bad vibes. I'll be much happier when we head for home.

"Enough of me. Tell me more about your life," Vito asks.

Steve and I repeat our cover stories. I work as a secretary for an elementary school in Los Angeles. Steve's a tax accountant working for a software company. I can sense Vito mentally dismissing us as being unworthy of his attention.

More dishes are served, ending with fruit, then sweet pastries and ice cream. The conversation continues on general subjects with Vito being the perfect host.

Unworthy we may be, but he asks us a lot of questions about our lives.

It's good to see Steve lying smoothly. It's a pain dealing with a beginner and yet Howard may be right. I do see possibilities in him.

Later, Vito, with Sajuk accompanying him, escorts us back to our room. Steve and I hold hands again to keep up our pretense. We thank him profusely for the lovely evening.

Just as he's leaving, he says, "I understand you were on the third floor today. I should warn you that one couple has the entire floor reserved for privacy."

Wow, that came out of the blue. Has the entire evening been a lead up to this question?

"I'm sorry if I caused a problem. I thought there might be a balcony or someplace with a view of the water. I bought a new camera in your gift shop, and I wanted to get some pictures."

Vito nods. "Now you know there are not. It would be good if you would avoid that floor." He turns and leaves.

CHAPTER 14

Steve confronts me. "What was that about the third floor? You told me you weren't going to their room."

"I wasn't on the third floor. I never left the stairway. I just scouted it, but there were maids in the hall when I looked. The only person who saw me was Javier. I passed him in the stairwell on my way down. But why would he make a complaint?"

"Maybe he likes his privacy."

"Isn't that a bit extreme?"

"What could be so secret on the third floor?"

"I guess we'll have to find out. For now, let's send these pictures of Javier to your dad."

We head for Vito's office, located off an empty side corridor. Ifrah told us earlier that since the hotel was over a hundred years old, it had to be retrofitted for electricity and computers. Vito's office was the only location available for a guest computer. We find it on a counter and marked for guests use. I'm surprised how quiet it is in this part of the hotel. I guess most people retire early or are gathered on the patio dancing to a CD player. The song choices were eclectic, Perry Como, Elvis, The Stones, KD Lang, Celine Dion, and the Platters mixed with Kabuki Theater music and Chinese pop songs and Viennese waltzes..

Steve quickly puts Morgan's email into the guest computer and starts downloading the pictures of Javier and Karista at the pool.

"Hola."

I practically jump out of my shoes. I turn, using my body to block Steve and the computer screen from whoever it is.

But the room is empty except for us. I check with Steve. He shakes his head. There was no mistake. Someone said hello in Portuguese. The word is pretty universal.

Tentatively, I say, "Hola."

From the far corner in an alcove partially hidden by a couch comes "Hola," followed by a loud squawk. I approach to find Cecilia, Vito's parrot in a large cage covered with a sheet. I lift the corner carefully. Cecilia's even more beautiful close up.

"Pretty bird, pretty Cecilia," I croon to her.

As Steve finishes downloading the pictures, I find a box of bird treats and give her one. I do love animals, and it's all I can do not to open the cage door, and a window, and let her out. It's hard to tell if she could adjust to the wild after so many years in captivity.

How can someone like Vito, who claims he loves birds, lock them up in cages? I think about his obsession with his family's lost property. I guess he has possession issues.

"Done," Steve says. "Time to go."

As we head for the door, a man's voice drifts down the hall. "There's an office down here where we can get some privacy."

"That's Javier. Hide." We duck behind the couch near Cecilia.

"We have a right to be here," whispers Steve.

"Shh."

We hear Javier and two other people enter. Javier sits at Vito's desk and the others sit in the chairs across from him.

"We had a couple good days," a woman says with a French accent.

Steve recognizes the voice. "That's—"

I cover his mouth with my hand.

"Let's see what you've got, Francoise," Javier says.

"Not so fast," comes a man's deep voice.

"What's your problem? I have your money ready," responds Javier.

I risk a peek. The beggar and the French woman from the airport sit in front of Javier. No longer in rags, the beggar is a trim man wearing jeans and a tee shirt. He crosses his legs, displaying a pair of new, red Nike shoes.

Steve's eyes widen.

The beggar takes the offered money from Javier, but doesn't pass him the stack of credit cards and IDs resting on Francoise's lap.

"We'd like to talk about that. We want a bigger cut," the beggar says with an American accent.

"Oui," agrees Francoise.

"I already pay you double the going rate."

"It's not enough. We take all the risks." He accidentally bumps some of the cards out of Francoise's lap.

I can see Steve's face on one. It has his real name—Steve Harrison—and his Beverly Hills address. The cat could be out of the bag if Javier notices. I give a silent sigh of relief when he doesn't.

"You'd both still be rotting in jail if I hadn't bailed you out and trained you," he says.

Francoise hastily gathers the fallen credit cards. Steve's face disappears beneath the others.

"We figure we have more than paid you back," the beggar responds.

"It pains me to hear you've become greedy."

"We can find another buyer."

"You've made a most unfortunate choice." There's anger in Javier's voice.

Alarmed, Francoise says, "I'm sure we can come to an understanding."

"I understand you perfectly."

"Hola."

There's a moment of silence.

Drat that bird. Steve and I tense.

Will they come into the alcove to check? I slip the Glock from under my jacket. Steve surprises me by pulling a small antique dagger out of his pocket. Did he lift that off the wall? I'm impressed.

The beggar is the first to speak. "Who said that?"

Javier shrugs, "Don't be stupid. That's a parrot. Let's go."

To our relief, the three of them exit the office. Only when the sound of their footsteps recedes down the hall do Steve and I emerge.

"Pretty bird, pretty Cecilia." Cecilia mimics my voice perfectly.

We make a dash for our room. The only person we pass before we reach the lobby is the British guy with the penchant for knee socks. We practically knock him down as we race for the stairs.

Once in our room, Steve turns to me.

He manages to speak between gasps for air. "It was those people from the airport. That beggar, he was wearing my new Yeezys."

"And your cute French friend. Selling credit cards, passports, and IDs to Javier. Yours included. Looks like our boy is quite the international scammer. You realize Southeast Asia is huge in the black market passport business. Javier must be part of one of the syndicates that buys and sells them."

I guess that Andre was honest about why he's here in this hotel. Javier must be the go-to man for identity papers. Maybe Andre doesn't know about the Goya on the yacht.

"It's not good he has your ID with your real name and address. If he mentions it to Karista . . ."

"Can I call home and make the report?" he asks.

"Make sure they got the pictures."

#

I lie in bed thinking about what Grace told me about her missing sister. None of it is good.

Around three in the morning, I hear a soft rattle at the door from my bedroom to the veranda. Sorry, Andre. I don't want to see you again.

I hear a click as he pops the lock open. He pushes on the door. It won't budge. That's because I've propped a chair under the handle.

"Lexi?" He whispers through the tiny crack in the door. "Lexi, it's me."

I hold still and don't answer. It's the hardest thing I've ever done. I should hate him, but I can't. I was afraid this would happen if we ever came face to face. Logic and distance let me hate him. Now that my worst fear has happened, he's so close, my emotions are betraying me. It's pretty bad when the person you can't trust is yourself.

He waits a long time, quietly calling my name. And

then he's gone.

Goodnight, Andre, I say to myself. Saying that should make me feel good, but it doesn't.

I stare at the ceiling a long time before I finally fall asleep.

CHAPTER 15

I join Steve on the patio for breakfast. He wears another batik shirt that's so loud the glare makes me wince.

Vito stands near the kitchen. From here, he appears to be angrily questioning the staff as he waves his arms threateningly.

Steve notices, too. "Vito sure is pissed about something."

"So it seems." I suppress a smile.

"You were certainly up and out early."

"I didn't sleep well." I mention that Grace will be joining us and fill him in on her missing sister. Before I can share my fears about Emmy Lou, Grace joins us.

I introduce her to Steve.

"Any luck?" I ask.

"None," Grace says. "Maybe I got this whole thing

wrong. I'm not gettin' anywhere so I'm thinkin' of going home."

I try to reassure her, but my dark thoughts make me think she'd be safer going home.

"Grace," I ask, "does your sister by any chance have money?"

"We're not rich by any means, but we do have a small inheritance from our grandparents. Emmy Lou was using hers to travel. It was somethin' she always wanted to do.

That confirms my worst suspicions.

I notice Vito moving from guest table to table, asking questions. The guests are shaking their heads in response. When he reaches our table, his head swings from me to Grace and back. There's surprise in his glance, which he immediately covers up.

He kisses my hand, lingering over it way too long.

I introduce them, adding, "Vito is the owner of the hotel. You should ask him about your sister."

Grace does, but Vito denies all knowledge and suggests that perhaps she's mistaken and Emmy Lou never stayed there. Grace pulls out a picture of herself with her sister and shows it to him. He shakes his head no. He doesn't recognize her.

I notice the two sisters look very much alike. Was that why seeing Grace surprised him?

"I also am asking for information," he says. "Some vandals have opened the cages for several of my aves— excuse my Portuguese, I mean birds. They have escaped. I prize them highly. Have you seen someone near the cages?"

All three of us deny any knowledge. Vito excuses himself and moves on to the next table.

After breakfast, we pass Karista and Javier at the tour desk. According to a flyer, today's tour is an all-day affair that goes north to one of the small orangutan rescue stations.

As soon as they walk away, I check with the attendant. Javier and Karista are going.

No point to our sitting in the hotel if Karista isn't going to be here. Maybe I could use the time to check out their room, but that will have to wait. I think the best thing I can do is stay near Karista. I hurry off to catch up with Steve. The trip leaves in fifteen minutes. I still won't have time to tell him my suspicions about what may have happened to Grace's sister.

Grace decides to join us when she hears where we're heading. I encourage her since she isn't leaving until tomorrow, and I can keep an eye on her, too. I promptly sign Grace, Steve, and myself up. We get the last three spots.

By the time I locate Steve and grab a tote for my hat, the Glock, and my sunscreen, the first jeep containing Karista and Javier is already filled. I'm surprised to see there's a guard with a rifle. When asked, Ramelan informs us there are bandits and poachers in the region we're headed toward.

Steve, Grace, and I are in the second jeep, with the American couple and the twins. Lucky us.

Andre strolls out of the hotel, chatting with Vito just as we're leaving. He spots me in the second jeep, and I wave as we drive past. I receive a scowl in response.

We have a long drive through the jungle and out to the paved road before we turn north to our destination. According to the concierge, our trip will be to a small place that saves and trains baby orangutans before returning them to the wild. My kind of place. It should be interesting, but I only hope I can separate Javier and Karista long enough to have a chat with her.

As the drive drags on, the twins get restless. To help their Mother keep them busy, I ask them to see how many wild animals they can spot. The game turns out to be a success with the adults, too. Steve looks up as many as he can in his guidebook to share their proper names and details. After being bitten a few times by flying insects, I declare, to the twin's amusement, that they be reclassified as vampire bugs. As we drive, we can see the black smoke of one of Sumatra's many active volcanoes in the distance. There are rain clouds on the horizon, but they burn off as the day progresses.

Finally, we turn off the pavement and back into the jungle. The jeeps come to a stop near a hand-carved sign: "Orangutan Sanctuary." It's with relief we step out of the jeep and stretch.

The sanctuary is a small place with a dozen or so large

cages. Each with several infant or adolescent orangutans. Behind the small office is a deep, vertical ravine with a river cutting through the bottom far below.

Our guide welcomes us and gives us each a surgical mask to wear. He explains that it protects the orangutans from human diseases. He also tells us that orangutan means people of the jungle.

For the next hour, he shows us around and shares information about what they do at the sanctuary. The young orangutans fascinate me with their large eyes and shy, sweet smiles. They look exactly like human babies. Not a surprise since their DNA is 97 percent the same as humans. I wonder what it's like to have prehensile feet in addition to hands like they do.

The guide tells us that unlike many other animals, orangutans are taught by their mothers for nine to twelve years before they go off on their own. The role of the sanctuary is to fill in that education for the orphans so they can survive when they are released, which is the goal here. It's sad how endangered they are. Why would anyone want to harm such gentle creatures?

While the information is fascinating, I try several times to work myself close to Karista. Somehow, Javier always manages to place himself at her side. My guess is he doesn't want her to form any friendships where people might become suspicious if anything happens to her.

When the tour ends, Ramelan and the driver of the other jeep lay out a lovely picnic packed by the hotel near the ravine. After lunch, Ramelan announces we'll be leaving in half an hour.

I watch as Karista produces her sketch book and walks back near the cages at the sanctuary to draw the orphans. Once she seats herself and begins to sketch, I wander toward her. From the corner of my eye, I see Javier spot me and move to cut me off. In what almost becomes a race, I manage to sit down next to Karista first. Annoyed, Javier takes the other side.

"Hi," I say, including both of them. "I hear you're from California, too."

Javier frowns, but Karista smiles. "We are. What part are you from?"

"Sacramento," I lie in an effort to quiet any suspicions Javier might have.

"Los Angeles for me. Are you enjoying your trip?" she asks in a soft voice.

"Yes, it's lovely here. Are you an artist?"

"I guess you could call it my passion. These baby orangutans are adorable."

She sketches as she talks and one of the orphans comes to life on her pad.

She really is good. When I say so, she looks embarrassed.

"Thank you, but most of my classmates at school are better."

Having seen her work, I doubt it. She either doesn't realize how good she is or she's being modest. Wait.

Neither of those would describe my conception of Karista as a rich snob.

In fact, she appears shy. Darn. It looks like I'm going to have to change my opinion of her. First Andre, then Steve, and now Karista. One would almost think that I'm a bad judge of character. The distressing evidence continues mounting up to prove it.

"We should join the others," Javier says to Karista.

She doesn't raise her head from her drawing. "You go ahead, honey. I'll be along in a minute."

"It's okay. I'll wait with you."

She gives him a sweet smile, but doesn't stop sketching.

I know a stalemate when I see one. I'll have to try to get her alone another time.

I excuse myself and head back to the group, which is clustered near the edge of the ravine. I stand between Steve and Grace and look down the deep cliff at the river.

Two young Sumatran elephants are playing in the water below. Steve and others take pictures with their zoom lenses. There's lots of jostling in the group for better angles and movement to get a better view.

Suddenly, Grace screams as she erupts forward from the group and toward the ravine's edge. I manage to grab her arm as she goes by, but her impetus swings her body over the edge and lands me facedown, still hanging on to her. I can't manage her weight for long. Nor do I have the strength to pull her up by myself.

Rocks and dirt shower down the sheer wall. I try to dig my toes into the ground to stop myself as I'm drawn inexorably closer and closer to the edge, but the ground is too soft to get a good purchase. Still, there's no way I'm letting Grace go.

Abruptly, Grace's weight stops dragging me past the cliff edge. Looking down, I can barely make out a tiny outcropping that Grace's toes rest on. Thank goodness for that.

"Help," I call out. "Help!" The dirt under Grace is crumbling. Another second and we could both plunge to our deaths.

People are moving away in shock, but not closer to help. Then a hand passes me and locks onto Grace's arm next to mine.

"Swing your other arm up, Grace," Steve says from beside me. She manages to raise it and he grabs it.

Other people finally respond and latch onto Steve and me.

"Okay, that's good. Hang on Grace."

"Now pull," he instructs everyone. We do, and then there are more hands supporting us and reaching for Grace to drag her safely back onto level ground.

Away from the edge, Steve and I look at each other with relief. That was close. I hold Grace as she shakes and sobs with shock. The mother of the twins asks Ramelan to find some left over coffee from lunch and add some sugar to it. He brings it from the jeep and offers it to Grace, telling her that she must be more careful in the future.

As she drinks, I glance around. The armed guard and the other driver wait near the jeeps. Karista hovers nervously nearby. Javier stands apart from the concerned group around us and watches with his arms crossed. There's a stoic expression on his face. I wonder if he had anything to do with Grace's fall, or am I just ready to blame anything bad on him?

Steve and Ramelan help us to our feet. "Come," Ramelan says. "Let's head back."

The ride home is a subdued one. The scare put a damper on the otherwise pleasant day. Even the twins are silent and sleep most of the way home.

I manage a few quiet questions with Grace. She insists someone shoved her in the middle of her back. But was the shove accidental or not? She has no idea who did it, and there's no way to find out. I suggest she arrange to leave first thing in the morning and spend the night with Steve and me. I'd hate for her to have another "accident." One that might not end as well for her.

Dinner is underway when we reach the hotel. A classic Indonesian shadow puppet show follows the meal, which smells wonderful, but I'm too worried to do more than nibble.

Steve volunteers to give the couch to Grace for the night. I nix that and offer to share my bed with her. I don't think anything will happen while we're with her, but a crowd didn't stop today's attempt on her life. I just don't believe in taking any chances.

I look around our suite. I'm getting a bad vibe. Something's nagging me about our rooms. Something's different, but before I can really think about it, Grace takes a shower, and I finally catch a moment for a quick word with Steve.

"Have you heard about sweetheart swindles?"

"Is that the same as a Casanova con where one person romances somebody rich in order to steal their money?"

"It's a despicable crime. All the victim has to be is vulnerable and lonely. They don't have to be rich. A little savings, a steady paycheck is enough. Once the thieves steal, borrow, or are given all the target's obtainable money, they disappear. The victims are left heartbroken and impoverished. Sometimes even dead."

"Okay?"

"Normally the victims are middle-aged or older. I think that's what's happening here, but with younger women as targets. Grace said she and her sister inherited money from their grandparents. I think Emmy Lou met the wrong man on her travels in Japan. He brought her here and then stripped her of all her money and murdered her."

"Then Karista . . ."

I nod. "One of the first things a sweetheart swindler does is to isolate their victim from their families and loved ones. They do it by physical separation or by creating an antagonistic situation where the victim rejects the warnings of their family and friends.

122

Karista's father started asking questions about Javier and right away they leave on vacation to this isolated place. I think Grace is at risk, too, because she's been asking too many questions about Emmy Lou's disappearance. The swindler wants to put a stop to that. And, unless Karista is in it with him, I believe she's the next target."

"You mean Javier?"

"I do."

"What about Denise?"

The water turns off in the shower. I hush Steve. "We'll talk more later, but I want to be sure Grace leaves safely in the morning."

I should force him to go with Grace and get on a plane home. I've definitely changed my mind about Karista's safety and possibly ours. It's imperative I talk to her.

I glance around our room. Something still rattles my subconscious, but I'm too worried to figure out what it is.

Grace heads right for bed. Steve sacks out on the couch. I decide to take a nice soothing bath before I turn in. I wish it was that easy to eliminate the turmoil in my head.

I turn the bedroom lights off so Grace can sleep before I slide into the tub. It feels divine. The hotel's bath gel has a lovely floral smell. It's so relaxing, I let go and my mind drifts toward sleep.

A piercing scream wakes me. It's Grace.

I leap out of the tub. Rats, the Glock is in my bag in the

other room.

I flip on the light in the bedroom . . . and the tableau it reveals makes me laugh.

Grace sits up in bed, horrified. Under the covers next to her is Andre, apparently naked. The look on his face mirrors Grace's. Pure shock. Steve stands frozen in the doorway to the living room.

The situation is just too funny. My laughter makes Andre turn in my direction.

He points at Grace indignantly. "What's she doing here?"

Steve responds, "The question is what are you doing here?"

Both men turn their focus on me. Realizing I'm wet and naked, I duck back in the bathroom and grab my robe.

Grace snatches up a sheet for cover and scrambles out of bed.

"It's okay, Grace," I say. "He's harmless. He won't hurt you."

"I'm not sure I like being described as harmless," says Andre.

An hour later, as I'm drifting off to sleep, I'm still smiling. The sight of Andre's face when he realized Grace wasn't me is one I'll always treasure. That and Andre trying to hurriedly slip his pants on again. Even Steve was laughing by the time Andre grabbed his shirt and exited the room with all the dignity he could muster.

I felt bad for him—for about a split second.

After he left, I remembered what was different about the room when we returned from the tour.

The wooden chairs I'd used to prop against the doors to keep Andre out last night are missing. I'll bet that Andre paid the bellboy to have them removed while we were out. He needn't have bothered. I was so upset tonight, I totally forgot to use them.

Still, Andre's presence is a serious distraction I don't need. I can't put my finger on what's going on here yet. Why would anyone try to kill Grace except to silence her questions about her sister. And that begs the question -- what did happen to her sister? I can only hope Andre's not involved.

CHAPTER 16

Grace and I finish our coffee on the patio while we wait for the jeep to the airport to begin loading.

She looks around nervously. "I can't wait to get on that airplane."

I couldn't agree more. "It won't be much longer."

Over by the kitchen entrance, Vito yells himself hoarse at the staff. I'm sorry to see him taking out his problems on them.

Grace glances over at Vito and back. "I hear he's upset because someone let more birds go last night.

"Really?" I hide a smile.

Steve joins us. When Grace steps away to the ladies room, he tells me, "I just talked to Dad. Guess whose picture popped up on Denise's Internet sites."

I have no idea.

"Kevin's bodyguard, Nate. And he's admitted he was

seeing her secretly."

That's a total surprise.

"Police claim Kevin would have fired him if he knew Nate was seeing his daughter's roommate. The police are arguing that he must have killed her to keep Kevin from finding out. He's denying he had anything to do with it."

Can that be true? Are we wasting our time here? "Is there any evidence?" I ask.

He shrugs.

"I guess it could be true," I say. "Nate's capable of murder under the right circumstances or even in a rage-induced accident. But with a curved knife? Probably from here in Sumatra? I don't think so."

"Maybe he picked up the knife in the house. Like if Karista or her dad brought one home from their travels."

"I guess that is possible."

We both glance toward Karista and Javier seated a few tables away. I'm annoyed to see Javier staring right at us.

Karista has her back to me. Oddly, she's wearing the same yellow sundress, hat, and huge sunglasses she had on yesterday. Maybe she packed a limited amount of clothes. As a rich girl, I would have expected her to bring a steamer trunk. There's no fee for checked baggage for first class passengers on most planes. There's something else odd about Karista this morning, but Javier's stare distracts me. I look away.

That's a lot of animosity just because he saw me in the third floor stairwell. Why on earth would it worry him so much? If he's not Denise's murderer, the only question left is is he just Karista's possessive boyfriend or does he have designs on her money? But if he's running an identity fraud scam, we know he's a criminal. Either way, it's not safe to leave her here with him.

I've never felt as unfocused as I do on this trip. Either I'm losing my touch or Andre has totally messed with my head. I need to get a grip.

After coffee, I walk Grace out to the jeep, leaving Steve to keep an eye on Karista.

We say goodbye as Ramelan loads Grace's bags.

I tell her, "Don't forget to call me when you're in the airport. If you don't, I'll have to arrange a rescue party to find you." Grace nods. Nearby, another couple who's leaving, and Ramelan overhear me. They turn and give me funny looks. I feel silly, but I don't want anyone to think they can get away with grabbing her between here and the airport without it being noticed. I don't think that will happen, especially with another couple along, but who knows?

I watch the jeep as it drives out of sight. Grace should be safe now. I wish I could say the same about Steve, Karista, and me. I need to get us out of here, too.

I head back to the room to call Morgan to give him an update. I'm surprised to find another beautiful bouquet of branches with tiny yellow orchids. I notice the attached card has been opened. It reads: Dear Lexi, I enjoyed our dinner. May I hope for another one? Vito.

Hmm. I don't see any flowers for Steve. Did Vito not buy our 'we're a couple routine?' Maybe Steve has the right approach and we should work harder on that.

Howard answers at the bank when I call. I tell him my latest suspicions about Javier working a sweetheart swindle and why I think so. It's a relief to speak with him as he gets the idea quickly. I can leave it to him to fill in Morgan and Kevin.

"The facial recognition programs are running his pictures. No match yet."

"It's possible he's not in the database."

I know it can take days to get a match. I wish it were faster.

"Howard, there's another problem. Andre's here."

Silence from his end. And in that moment, I have a realization.

"You knew he was going to be here, didn't you?"

More silence. I know I'm right. How else would Andre know things about me that are recent, like what kind of gun I use? Or that I was even coming here?

"How long have you and Andre been in contact?"

Suddenly there's noise on the line.

"Sorry Lexi, the line's breaking up . . ."

"Don't be so ridiculous. Stop tapping on your phone," I yell angrily. "This isn't funny."

Too late. He hung up. What a rat. Why would he give Andre information about me? He knows how I feel about him. I respect Howard a lot. There must be something behind this. I just wish I knew what.

I shove the phone into my bag so I'll have it nearby when Grace calls. Andre and Howard. As pissed as I am, I can't let them distract me from Karista.

I find Steve on the patio finishing his breakfast. The boy eats like a horse. I sit and order another coffee.

"Did you see the flowers in the room?" Steve asks between bites.

I nod.

"You notice he didn't invite me. I think the man likes you."

"Yes, but is that a good thing or a bad thing?"

Andre slips into the seat beside me. "Good morning all."

Steve practically snarls, but his mouth is too full of food to say anything.

Andre continues, "I wanted to catch you early, Lexi. What does a guy have to do to have a private"—he shoots an annoyed look at Steve—"conversation with you?"

Steve swallows as fast as he can..

"I just spoke with Howard," I say.

"Howard who?"

"Give it up, Andre. I understand the two of you have been talking."

"Oh, that Howard. Nice man. Did you say hello for me?"

"I did."

The conversation has lost Steve, but he can tell

something's up. He sits quietly and listens.

"Poor old Howard. It's sad to hear his mouth has sprung a leak. Did much dribble out?"

"Nothing actually, but thank you for confirming my suspicions. Why don't you come by our room tonight. We can discuss it. You already know the way."

"Tonight? I'm not sure I'm available. I'll have to check my schedule."

"Tonight. Take it or leave it."

"Are you planning on locking the doors again?"

"They'll be open—for tonight only."

He gives Steve another look. "It's hardly private."

"Best I can offer."

"I'll take it."

"Andre. Clothing is required."

The waiter comes by and takes his order.

"How was your tour yesterday? I heard there was some unpleasantness," Andre continues when the waiter leaves.

Before I can respond, there's a commotion from the direction of the lobby. I stretch my neck to see the cause. A couple of men in uniform crowd in the doorway with Vito.

Police?

Alarmed, I turn toward Andre and nod toward the police. His eyes widen momentarily, then his face goes blank.

Vito leaves the police to hurriedly approach Javier and whisper to him. Javier looks in the direction of the uniforms, nods to Vito. He rises, and offers his arm to

Karista. The two of them amble in the direction of the lobby with Vito following.

Shoot. I have to see what's going on. I drop my napkin and stand. Amazingly, Andre's disappeared. I didn't even hear the scrape of his chair. It must be his normal reaction when the police show up.

I head for the other entrance to the lobby. When I get there, I pause in the doorway to see which way Javier, Karista, and the police went. They're moving to the far corner of the lobby.

Karista and Javier settle into seats with the men in uniform sitting opposite them. Vito hovers unhappily nearby.

Steve crashes into my back just like at the airport.

"Quit doing that," I hiss at him.

"Let me escort you, Auntie. It might be a good time to double check on possible travel arrangements."

The boy is definitely quick on the uptake. He takes my arm and we stroll toward the reception desk.

"Good morning, Ifrah. Could you check the plane schedules to Singapore for us?" Steve asks.

She brings up the flights on her computer and reads them off.

I miss most of it because I'm trying to hear the conversation across the lobby. I give up after a few minutes. Their voices are too low.

Closer to the group are the British couple, studying the wall of bronze weapons. I'd love to trade places with them.

They stand close enough to overhear the conversation.

"What kind of uniforms are those gentlemen wearing?" I ask, indicating the policemen.

"They are the police from Medan," Ifrah says.

"Is that couple in trouble?" I nod toward Karista and Javier.

"No trouble. They're here to ask questions for the American police.

"I'm glad there's no problem."

Steve and I move into another seating area to watch the action. Everything looks amicable. Javier appears to be doing the talking for Karista and himself. Vito orchestrates the appearance of coffee and snacks for the officers. Again I can only see Karista's back. She nods her head occasionally in agreement with Javier.

"I wish we could be a fly on that wall," I whisper to Steve.

"Me, too. They must be here about Denise. Should we move closer?"

"No. It would be too obvious." I pretend to read a magazine. Hopefully I've got it right-side up this time. Steve lies back and half-closes his eyes, giving the impression he's dozing.

After fifteen minutes, the policemen put down their cups. They stand to shake hands all around. With a few more words and smiles, they leave. I hear their vehicle start out front. After a moment, it departs.

Steve whispers, "Looks like that went okay. They must

be satisfied with Javier's and Karista's answers."

"According to body language, Javier definitely controlled that interview." I glance back over to see Javier and Vito having an intense conversation.

"I wonder what that's about," I say.

"Maybe Vito doesn't enjoy the police coming to his hotel."

"If the police are asking questions about Denise, it bothers me that Karista had no reaction to the news."

"What do you mean?" Steve says.

"From her body language, she showed no surprise, no shock, and no sign of being upset."

He thinks about it a moment. "You're right."

Karista stands and heads for the stairs.

Funny, the pretty yellow dress doesn't fit quite as perfectly as it did yesterday. She gives it a tug to pull it into place. Looks like she put on a few pounds, too. That's silly. She couldn't possibly have done that since yesterday. Uh, oh. The only explanation terrifies me.

I grab Steve's arm and whisper, "Steve, meet me upstairs in our room.

His mouth is open as I hurry away.

I pass Andre standing near the stairs.

He takes one look at my tense face and grabs my arm, "Lexi, what is it?"

"Later." I wrench my arm back and rush up the stairs.

He calls after me, "You know, seeing you again isn't going the way I envisioned it."

Once in my room, I dump my bag's contents on the bed. Of course what I'm looking for comes out last—the sat phone. I dial as fast as I can. It's ringing . . .and ringing. Come on Howard. Be there. And ringing . . .

"Lexi?" Morgan answers.

I've never been so glad to hear his nasal voice in my life.

"Morgan. We've hit a problem. The local police arrived to interview Karista and Javier. We think it was about Denise for the American police, but Karista wasn't here. There was an imposter wearing her clothes and pretending to be her. We don't know where Karista is."

"You lost her? You told me she was fine."

"I'm hanging up. We'll find her."

"Keep Steve out of—" I hang up.

Steve hurries in. "What's going on?"

I fill him in as quickly as I can. He's appalled.

"I just assumed that was Karista."

I'd assumed, too, so I don't bother to point out the old saying about the word assume. That it makes an ass out of you and me. I could kick myself.

"So now what?" Steve asks.

Indeed, that's the question. I sink onto the couch.

"First, we need to find out if Karista is still alive. And it won't hurt to get a picture of the woman pretending to be her."

"Give me the camera. I can get a photo."

"Be careful and find me afterward. I'll check out the

hotel and grounds for a Karista." There's only a limited number of places she could be held captive. She'd have to be hidden from the guests and the staff. The most obvious place is the third floor, but I decide to avoid that for now. It won't do to have a head on confrontation Javier.

"What if she's already—"

"Stop. Don't even think it."

I hate involving Steve in this. It could get ugly, with options like death or life in a Sumatran prison. Neither is a choice I want us to face. Later, I'll insist he leaves on tomorrow's airport run.

"What about a second gun? Will Van der Meer loan you another?"

I shake my head. "Let's not count on him. I'm not sure how close he is to Javier. He may have come here to buy fake identity papers from him, so keep what we know to yourself." Then I remember. "Last night, where did you get that knife?"

"Off the wall display downstairs. You have a gun. I wanted something in case I needed it."

The boy is definitely earning bonus points from me lately. He leaves in pursuit of the fake Karista. I head downstairs to the hall near Vito's office. I pause a moment to check inside, but it's empty. Even Cecilia's cage is vacant. I move down the hall and open the next door I come to. It's a supply closet.

I'm abruptly grabbed from behind and spun around.

My heart pounds. Oh, thank goodness. It's Andre.

"You have to stop giving me heart attacks."

"What are you doing?"

"Why are you following me around?"

"Do you honestly need me to tell you?"

I turn away.

"Something's come up."

"Care to explain?"

"I . . . no, I don't," I stammer.

His face goes cold. "What is it with you? You know how I feel."

The sat phone rings in my bag.

"Don't answer it. Talk to me."

"I have to." I answer the call. It's Grace. She's in the international section of the airport. She's fine. I hang up and turn back to Andre.

He's already halfway down the hall. Half of me wants to call him back and tell him everything. The other half knows I can't take the risk.

CHAPTER 17

I skip the public rooms in my search for Karista. They're not a logical place to hold a hostage. I refuse to believe she's dead, but I can't shake the possibility out of my heart. Am I to blame? I should have spoken to her directly and not been put off by Javier's interference or Nate's arrest.

My hunt takes me into the food preparation areas. The kitchen staff pays me no mind. Not even when I check in the storeroom and peek into the walk-in freezer. I can imagine them muttering, "Crazy foreigners." I pass out of the kitchen and open all the doors I come across.

The first one is a wine and alcohol room. Next, steam pours from the laundry room. Baskets of dirty linen line the walls outside its door. I dig through the biggest ones, afraid to admit to myself that I'm searching for a body. Thank goodness I find nothing but sheets and towels.

I come across more closets filled with hotel supplies and cleaning equipment and a break room with lockers for employees, but no place private enough to hide Karista or her body.

Since there's no basement, I head outside to the workmen's compound. I find all the utilities are there, concentrated in two structures: a shed for the grounds men—trash bins with empty wine and liquor bottles nearby—and a large ramshackle garage for auto and equipment repairs. Nothing out of the ordinary except for the questioning glances I get from a couple gardeners. Yet I have the creepiest feeling that someone's watching me.

I pause at the gate on the far side of the compound. To my right, the bay looks quiet in the afternoon sun. From here, the dark, dense jungle is only about three hundred feet away in front of me and it curves around the hotel in a U-shape with only a break for the road. If Karista or her body is in the jungle or in the bay, we may never find her.

I should have moved quicker. At least she would have known there were friends nearby. Twenty-four hours ago she looked so happy. I've never been responsible for protecting someone before. And I've totally failed. Poor Karista.

Remorse overwhelms me. I sink onto a bench.

Someone slides onto the seat beside me. I don't have to look to know who it is. Andre enfolds me into his arms and holds me tight.

His presence is soothing. He places an arm around me

and pulls me close. We sit in silence.

"I should have let him fire me," I say.

"Your boss at the bank?"

"How do you know I work for a bank?" Oh right, Howard. "Did Howard tell you why we're here?"

"Only that you were checking up on some girl. I take it she's the one with Javier."

He doesn't miss much. I had better take my own advice and not say anything to him.

"Is she why you've been wandering around the hotel?"

"Yes."

"Where haven't you looked?"

I indicate the jungle and the bay. "There."

"Let's hope not," Andre says. "No reason she'd be in the jungle, is there?"

After a moment, he adds, "Give me a big city any day. There's a reason most Homo sapiens left the jungle, and I salute them for an excellent decision."

I have a sudden thought. What if Javier is greedy? He knows Karista's father has money. He might demand a ransom for her. If so, he'll need to keep her alive for proof of life. And that will give me time to find her. Thank goodness. But I better be fast. I know Javier won't release her even if the ransom is paid. I've got to call Morgan to prepare him.

I leap to my feet. Andre stands and grabs my hand.

"Wait." He kisses me, but all I can think of is Karista. I try to pull away, but he holds me tight.

"Let go."

"Lexi, wait, We need to talk."

"Not now. I've got to make a call."

Reluctantly, he releases my hand. "What's with you and the phone? Can't it wait?"

"I shake my head and race into the hotel."

Be careful, Cherie. Your boss should never have sent you here."

Back in the room, I dial the sat phone as rapidly as I can. The line rings once and Morgan picks up.

"Where have you been? I've been trying to reach you for hours."

"What's going on?"

"You lost Karista and then you pull a damn disappearing act."

I notice he doesn't mention he couldn't reach Steve, either.

"What's happened there?" Please, please be a ransom demand. Please.

"Kevin called the FBI to report her disappearance."

"No ransom demand? Listen, Morgan, there may be one. Get the FBI to put a tap on all Kevin's phones immediately and make sure Kevin insists on proof of life. Steve's trying to get a picture of the woman pretending to be Karista. Any luck identifying Javier?"

"Not yet. I can't believe you totally screwed this up. I want Steve out of there immediately—"

I hang up before his rant can escalate. When I do, I

catch an odd smell in our room. It takes me a second to identify—pipe smoke. Odd. The only person I've seen with a pipe is the British guy with the knee socks. Maybe the smoke came in through the veranda doors.

I go search for Steve. Hopefully, he's had better luck than I have.

I find him in the lobby chatting with Ifrah. He sees me and follows me out the front door. The staff is lighting the red lanterns for the evening.

We find a secluded area with a bench. In the distance, dark storm clouds head in our direction. Looks like we're in for rain tonight.

"Did you get it?" I ask.

"Yes, but I couldn't get too close. She never removed that hat or those huge sunglasses. I slipped into Vito's office and sent the ones I got with a note. She and Javier just went up to the third floor.

I nod. I look around again to be sure we're alone. Then I fill him in on the FBI and why Karista might still be alive.

"Then the pictures are even more critical."

I agree.

We decide to search the third floor tonight.

As we consider a plan of action, one of the tour jeeps returns from the day's outing. We glance up as the guests emerge.

One of the young couples step out first. They're rapturously talking to each other in German about a bird of paradise they saw. Next is the family with two young boys. They look miserable. I guess two days confined in a jeep for hours has left them cranky and out of sorts.

By the time the last tourist emerges, we're no longer paying much attention. Suddenly Steve gasps, and I turn.

It's Karista. The real one. She's carrying her sketch pad.

I look at Steve, speechless.

Karista smiles and chats easily with the guide. "Thank you so much for a lovely day. I can't believe we saw a Sumatran tiger. And the birds, they were magnificent." She turns toward the hotel just as Javier emerges. They hug. Javier notices us. He throws a look of distaste in our direction, takes Karista's arm, and escorts her inside.

I feel like someone kicked me in the stomach with steel-toe boots. Steve is as dumbfounded as I am. How could we have been so wrong? What did we see this morning? Why was someone wearing Karista's clothes?

CHAPTER 18

Dinner is a gloomy affair for Steve and me, even though I've put on my favorite deep blue dress. The one with the V-neckline and the knee-length skirt that moves well when I walk. Normally it makes me feel good about myself, but tonight I'm conflicted. Thank goodness Karista is fine. But I've been so wrong about everything. Maybe I should go for that career flipping burgers when we get back. I'm certainly not succeeding at this one. It will take more than my favorite dress to lift my spirits tonight.

I hold my wine glass up to the waiter for another refill. Steve raises his, too. I know I'm drinking more than I should, but why not? I can't screw things up more than I already have. I notice Steve matches me glass for glass. The food comes and goes without any remembrance of what I ate or if I ate. I pass on dessert and order another round of drinks.

I'm still reeling from my talk with Morgan when I called to tell him that Karista was okay.

His furious response included, "Are you on drugs?"

Apparently, he wasn't any kinder to Steve this time. The words weren't said, but it's pretty clear I'm fired. Luckily, and I use that word in only a relative sense. The FBI, personified by some smart-ass guy named Clark, told Kevin he wants us to keep an eye on Karista until he arrives in twenty-four hours to take over. Until then, we're not supposed to do anything that might attract attention.

Kevin must have pull with the FBI, too. I just wish he'd gone to them first and left me out of it. I'm up the proverbial creek without a paddle as far as knowing what to do. I follow people's money for a living, not them.

I'll have to warn Andre so he can pull his well-practiced disappearing act before Clark gets here. Come to think of it, where is Andre? He missed a great dinner of whatever it was.

I glance across the dining room at Karista and Javier. It's easy to spot them because of the usual circle of hovering waiters. I guess he must be a very generous tipper.

Is it still possible she's in this with him and not a victim? Am I totally wrong about Javier running a sweetheart scam? I know about a quarter of all serial killings are actually done by two men or a man and a woman. How did Denise end up dead? Did Karista deliberately disappear before the local police came this morning? Or was it arranged by Javier without her knowledge?

So many questions with no answers. What is their game? Whatever they're doing, it's pissing me off. I've waited too long as it is. I want some answers.

Screw Morgan and Clark. Screw being a place holder for the FBI and waiting for them to take over. I'm going to get some information tonight.

Steve lifts his glass again for the waiter. This time, I catch his eye and shake my head no. When the waiter arrives, I order black coffee for us both.

The dining room lights flicker and come back on. The storm is getting closer. Wind gusts through the open doors to the patio. Momentary chaos ensues as waiters rush to secure the doors and guests from the patio hustle back inside.

I have a sudden thought. "Was that woman from the airport, Francoise, the one who was dressed in Karista's clothes this morning?"

"I never got a good look, but it could have been. She's the right height and has a similar build. Should we call Dad?"

"Not yet. Let's see what we can find out."

We decide to go ahead with our search of the third floor. When we climb the stairs, we find a guard who looks like a male relative of Vito's bodyguard, sitting squarely at the top. He waves us away in no uncertain terms.

I consider taking him on, but it wouldn't accomplish

anything and would expose us to Javier. Steve and I retreat to our room. Time for a new plan. I refuse to be stopped.

Outside, the storm breaks. Rain pounds against the building in a torrent. The monsoon has arrived.

CHAPTER 19

Midnight. All's quiet in the building as the storm has knocked out the power. The other guests and staff retired early to bed. That's a plus for us. Outside the storm continues to drive rain against the hotel.

Dressed in black with my hair tucked under a stocking that's over my face, I slip silently out of our dark room into the deep shadows of the wet veranda. I have my bed sheet tied around my waist. Stockings are something I never wear for what they're designed for. I have to buy them especially for excursions like this one. Similarly dressed, Steve follows. I tried to talk him into waiting in the room, but he insists on coming.

I can't even guess what's inside all those empty rooms on the third floor.

"Remember to be quiet," I caution Steve. "The guard is in the hall. Javier and Karista are in their room on the other side of the hall, hopefully asleep. The biggest danger will be if Francoise and her partner are sleeping in a room upstairs and we stumble into them."

At the corner of the veranda, he boosts me up the post to where I can grab the bottom of the slippery railing on the floor above. Then it's a simple matter of pulling myself up. Once on the third floor, I duck under the veranda roof.

There, I untie the sheet wrapped around my waist, then fasten it to the corner post, and drop it down for Steve. He scrambles up the sheet and over the railing, then pulls the sheet up. We leave it tied to the post in case we need it for a quick escape.

The veranda stretches in front of all the rooms on this side of the third floor. We're on the opposite side of the hotel from room 314.

Where to start? Vito said Karista and Javier rented the entire third floor. That means all the rooms are supposed to be empty except for the one that Javier and Karista actually occupy. We may as well begin with the closest. I hand Steve a pair of latex gloves and put some on myself.

"Do you always carry these?" Steve whispers.

"They often come in handy." From his expression, I can bet that in the future, he'll always have gloves and stockings in his suitcase, too.

With Steve off to the side, I knock lightly on the veranda door just in case someone is inside. Hopefully, it's too soft for the guard on the stairs to hear. No response. I try the handle. It's locked. Not a problem. I studied the locks on our door below. They're the kind that a credit card opens easily by slipping it between the lock and the door jamb. I do that now, quietly looking in. All clear. Once inside, I close the heavy drapes to block any signs of our pocket flashlights. They're another item I always carry.

The room is musty, like it hasn't been aired in a while.

Steve whispers, "If you saw the maids on this floor, they should be fired. This room hasn't been cleaned in ages."

Definitely strange. The room must have been in use before Karista and Javier? But it takes a long time for a room to develop this kind of odor. And when we checked in and asked for a second room, we were told none were available. I can't imagine a hotel turning down income when there's an unused room open. Even with Javier paying for them, the hotel is losing money for all the extras like food, tips, and tours.

Steve and I go over everything carefully. We check under the bed, open the dresser drawers. I have no idea what exactly it is that we're looking for. It's one of those "I'll know it when I see it" things.

The last thing we do is open the closet. Inside is a stack of unmatched suitcases. That's odd. Why would a guest room be used as a storage room?

I unlatch the first case. It's filled with women's clothes. On top is a revealing negligee, size six. Steve opens the second case. Women's clothes again, only in size twelve.

We open each in turn. All the suitcases contain trendy, upscale, young women's clothes, but they're each filled with various sizes. Even their labels are in different languages. Different sizes, different women? This many women wouldn't have left their luggage behind. The suitcases appear stripped of anything that might identify the owners. It's just plain creepy.

We carefully replace the suitcases in the closet in the same order.

Done with this room, we move on to the next. Again, there's a musty odor. This time, we check the closet first. It's empty. So is the rest of the room. We move on to the third. It's directly across from Karista's and Javier's.

Another unused guest room, I think. Weird.

I start my search with the bureau. Nothing. Steve wanders about the room. "Here," he whispers. I join him as he points to two suitcases with the monogrammed initials FA partially scratched out and a filled plastic garbage bag hidden under the bed.

A sudden series of lightning strikes makes us jump nervously.

I drag the plastic bag out, smothering a cough from the dust that rises. Inside the bag, on top of expensive feminine clothes, size four this time, lies a tooth brush, a gold bracelet, a fancy Japanese camera, and elegant make-up jars.

No woman would leave this stuff behind, much less so many women.

I flip the bracelet over and find an inscription in Japanese.

Steve mouths, "Can you read that?"

I nod, shocked by what I'm reading. It says Happy 21st Fumiko, Love Mom and Dad. I mouth later to Steve and slip the bracelet in my pocket.

We carefully replace anything we moved, including returning the bag and suitcases to their place. As we do, I notice something else sticking out from under the bed. I pull on it. It's a third suitcase.

Steve flips the catches. Inside are women's clothes and toilet articles. We sort through them. Steve finds a written, but unmailed, hotel postcard hidden in a sweater pocket.

It's addressed to Grace Tyler in Daytona Beach, Florida. It reads:

Hi Sis,

That nice guy I met in Singapore? He's the best. We even enjoy the same bands. We came to this fabulous hotel in Sumatra. You'll have to come sometime. It's great. Hugs and kisses, Emmy Lou.

Steve and I exchange a horrified look as we realize it's from Grace's sister. I immediately put it in my pocket.

We find two more pieces of luggage stashed under the bed among the dust balls. Steve looks at me. "How many do you think . . . "

"We'll probably never know."

"I'll check the closet."

I head into the bathroom. It's bare except for linen. The

medicine cabinet behind the mirror is empty, too.

A gagging sound comes from the bedroom. I rush in to find Steve dry heaving—his eyes wide in horror.

"What?"

He indicates the closet. I jerk the door open.

Inside, grotesquely staring back, are Francoise and the beggar, wrapped in plastic and hanging from hooks. Very dead.

I notice Steve's red Yeezys dangling uselessly on the beggar's feet and then the bullet hole in the center of Francoise's forehead. The bodies are still warm. They can't have been there long.

Steve staggers for the bathroom and retches his dinner into the john. I put my arm around him in support.

"Just keep your head down," I whisper. "It will pass."

I wet a washcloth and hold it against his forehead.

Then I pour cold water on another and put it to my forehead. I'm feeling queasy, too.

I need to be smart about this. Clark will be here in the morning. Time to check my ego and let the feds take over.

Steve gives me a sick look. We need to get out of here.

We move into the bedroom and head for the veranda door.

Crash! The hall door bursts open.

The guard from the stairway enters, his gun aimed at us. "Raise hands."

We raise our hands.

The guard talks into a walkie-talkie. "I catch persons in

rooms."

Javier's voice comes back, "On my way up."

"Remove face," the guard orders.

Static comes from the walkie-talkie. The guard instinctively glances at it.

I jump him. We crash to the floor. Run," I manage to hiss at Steve. He doesn't move.

The guard's gun slides out of my reach. He pins my arms under me and reaches for his weapon. Not good. I manage to roll the guard over. A quick right cross takes him down.

I stagger to my feet and slam the door to the hall closed and lock it. Steve helps me push the bureau in front of it. I can hear footsteps racing up the hall toward us. The door won't hold Javier out for long.

Behind me, the guard has already regained consciousness and draws his knife.

Javier pounds on the door. "Open up."

As I turn, the guard rushes me, pinning me against the wall, his knife at my throat.

"I get him," yells the guard.

I twist my body and bury my knee in his groin.

He bends over in agony.

Steve whacks him on the head with a piece of bronze statuary. Lights out for the guard. He crumples to the floor. Good job, Steve!

Bam! Bam! Javier pounds on the door. "What's going on in there?"

Kicking the knife under the bed, I race for the veranda.

Ka-bam! Javier crashes his shoulder against the door. It doesn't budge.

Steve and I are out of the room and back to the sheet. Letting him go first, I release the sheet and slide down the corner post behind him.

Crash! Bam! We hear the dresser topple over in the room above us. Followed by the sound of the third floor room's door banging open against the wall and footsteps racing to the railing. I grab the sheet and run.

It's raining hard. The noise helps cover our retreat. Hugging the wall so as not to be seen from above, we dash down the second floor veranda to our room. We lock the door quickly and quietly behind us.

In the dark, I snatch off my stocking mask and whisper to Steve, "They may make a search. Ditch your clothes, turn some music on, and pour some champagne. Put a robe on. Pretend we've been here all evening."

I hurry into the bedroom and close the door. I can hear our pursuers pound up our veranda. They're testing the doors as they go. I freeze as our doorknob is twisted back and forth. The lock holds.

"Burgling anyone I know, Cherie?" Andre whispers from behind me.

CHAPTER 20

Andre's voice makes me jump ten feet. Javier doesn't need to kill me tonight. Andre will give me a heart attack first.

I try to flip on the light, but the power is still off. I can barely make out Andre beside me, sipping from a wine glass. So much has happened that I totally forgot I'd agreed to talk to him tonight. Make that last night.

"You're a little late."

He shrugs. "I've always been a night person. You better get out of those clothes and slip into bed before they come back."

That's good advice. I hastily duck into the bathroom, remove my clothes, and slip into a nightie. Back in the bedroom, I slide under the covers. I turn to find Andre slipping in behind me and removing his shirt.

Out in the hall I hear someone knocking on the guest

room doors and angry voices from protesting guests.

Suddenly, I hear our living room door burst open, followed by Javier's voice, yelling at Steve. Steve protests, but Javier flings the bedroom door open and bursts in with a flashlight.

A crack of lightning illuminates the room. I scream, playing my role, but I'm not faking. I no longer have any question that this Javier is a killer. If Francoise and the beggar weren't proof enough, Javier enters our room with a serpentine shaped knife clenched in his hand. The fierce expression on his face revealed by the few seconds of lightning will join my nightmares for the rest of my life.

Javier pauses when he recognizes Andre and lowers his knife.

"What the hell do you think you're doing?" Andre bellows.

Javier backs out. "Please accept my apologies. There's an intruder in the hotel."

Behind Javier, Steve's furious to discover Andre's presence.

Javier closes the bedroom door behind him as he leaves.

Out in the living room, I hear Steve protesting with Javier. "You can't just burst in here ...."

"Does your life always veer into farce?" Andre asks me.

I hastily avoid his arms. When I stand, I see a nasty scratch on my arm. Thank goodness it's not too deep. The guard must have caught me with the tip of his knife.

Spotting the scratch, Andre quickly removes a pillow case. He goes into the bathroom and returns with a wet towel and soap. He cleans the wound, pours wine into it, and gently binds it with strips from the pillow case.

"You used to take better care of yourself."

"It's nothing."

"You know better than to be careless about a wound in a tropical country." He finishes fastening the makeshift bandage. "I wanted to tell you how lovely you looked earlier tonight. I saw you at dinner."

Hmmm. I didn't see him.

"I remember when you first wore that dress in Sydney. We had dinner at that little restaurant near the Harbor Bridge."

I weaken toward him for a moment. "I remember. That was a long time ago." How I'd loved him then. How uncomplicated our relationship had been. At least I'd thought it was.

He continues, "Then we strolled over to the opera house. On the way, you took your sandals off and we danced barefoot in that fountain with all those chubby stone cherubs."

"The street musicians played Waltzing Matilda." It was a magical night. I was so happy then.

He presses closer and circles me with his arms and pulls me tight. I can't deny my attraction to him. Our eyes lock. Our lips move closer. And closer.

I break away, uncertain.

Andre still senses triumph in my uncertainty and moves nearer. I hold him off.

"You never give up, do you?"

"On you? Never. I know how sweet you are under all those prickly defenses."

The bedroom door swings open as Steve storms in. Andre throws up his arms in exasperation.

"What's he doing here?" Steve demands.

"I was invited," Andre says.

"It's time for you to leave."

"Lexi? I don't like leaving you alone," Andre says.

Steve turns beet red, but stands his ground. "She's not alone. I'm here."

Andre gives him a dismissive look.

"Now," Steve demands.

"He's right," I say. "You better go."

Andre puts his shirt on with exaggerated slowness. Steve fumes.

Andre says to him, "I forgive your churlishness because you have excellent taste in women."

"You don't need to tell me that."

"She has no idea how attractive she is. That's one of the things I love about her."

"Hey, I'm standing right here. Knock it off. Andre, word of warning. The FBI will be here sometime tomorrow."

"It's come to that, has it? Thank you, Cherie, but I'm

160

not leaving you here," he glances at Steve, "without protection."

Steve's face turns an unbecoming shade of red.

Andre saunters toward the veranda door.

"And Cherie, I wouldn't plan on releasing any more birds in the morning. Vito's arranged for an armed guard." He blows me a kiss before disappearing out into the dark.

"You're the one pissing Vito off? What are you thinking?" Steve's voice cuts through my thoughts.

"Healthy birds don't belong in cages."

"So, are you going to tell me?"

"Tell you what?"

"What's going on between you two?"

"None of your business. Now quit with the anger. We have more important things to talk about."

He collapses into a chair. "What are we going to do?"

"First, call the police," I say, "then call the desk, ask for Vito, and make a complaint about Javier busting in our room. It will look odd if we don't."

He picks up the room phone. "It's dead."

"Try the sat phone."

He does. "Static. Must be the storm. Looks like the battery's low, too."

"Just when we need it."

I'll go down to the desk and see if Vito has a ham radio or something."

"See if he'll come back with you. We'll have to tell him what we found, but let's do it privately. Ask Ifrah when the power will be back on."

Steve pulls his clothes on and leaves. I like that. He didn't ask any questions, he just follows instructions.

I drop onto the bed, relieved to be alone and have time to think. Thoughts of Andre go into a compartment of my brain, and I bang the door shut. I wish I could do that with my feelings, too. They're something I'll have to deal with later. And Karista? It's paramount to find out if she's involved. If not, my priority is to get her and Steve out of here safely. If she is, I'll gladly hand her over to Agent Clark tomorrow. There's no way I'll help a murderer, ever.

Steve enters. "I yelled at the night clerk about the disturbance. Poor guy. Must be ten other guests doing the same thing. That British guy was down there in his matching bathrobe and knee socks. I guess he wears them to bed. No luck on Vito. He left for supplies this afternoon before the storm. Won't be back until tomorrow. The night clerk said there's no radio or means of communication."

I turn to Steve. "Upstairs you asked about the Japanese inscription on the gold bracelet. I remove it from my pocket and read, "Happy twenty-first birthday, Fumiko. Love, Mom and Dad."

Steve doesn't get the significance.

"Did you hear about the Japanese heiress who went missing about six months ago?"

Now he gets it. "She was never found. All her money disappeared from her bank in a series of off-shore wire transfers. All her credit cards were maxed out, too."

"Her name was Fumiko."

"You think the bracelet was hers?"

I nod my head. "Japanese are big targets for credit card fraud. As a group, they have the highest limits on their cards. Javier is an equal nationality scammer. When we leave here, I'm going to mail this to her parents with an explanation of where we found it. Hopefully, it will give them some closure."

Steve shakes his head as if to make the horror of the night go away. He sits down abruptly.

"Why did he kill them?"

"I'm guessing Francoise and the beggar didn't get their raise. Pissing off Javier doesn't seem to end well."

Steve rests his head in his hands.

"Remember," I say, "we're only guessing that it was Javier. And none of this looks good for Karista,"

"I thought Javier was running a sweetheart scam for her money," he says. "But with all those suitcases upstairs, Grace's sister . . . those women can't all be victims?"

I slowly nod again. "And probably all dead."

#

I can't sleep. When I close my eyes, Javier's furious face pops into my head, along with flashes of curved knives covered in blood, and I wake in a cold sweat.

I decide fresh air will help even though the rain continues. As I open the veranda doors, I'm shocked to find Andre. He's fast asleep in a wooden chair against the railing.

Not too fast asleep. His eyes pop open at the sound of my doors and his hand goes to the gun in his lap.

He gives a half smile when he sees me.

"Making sure that you're safe."

"Come," I say. "You can sit inside."

CHAPTER 21

The usual guests are on the patio for a cold breakfast since the power is still off. Among them, Vito's father, Alfonso, who reads a paper as he eats. Right-side up, I notice. I wave at him and mouth the words thank you, referring to his arranging our tour of his son's yacht.

The British couple looks like they're having a quiet disagreement. The twins run around playing tag as their indulgent parents eat. Javier's and Karista's table awaits their usual late arrival. It's amazing how disconnected I feel from them all—like I'm outside a window looking in through the glass.

I check the bay. Vito's yacht still hasn't returned. Rats. We really need his support. Or do we? I have questions about him, too.

I glance up and see Karista arrive by herself. This might be my chance. I move to her table and slip, uninvited, into Javier's seat.

"Hi, there. I saw you come back from the jungle tour yesterday. Did you enjoy it?" I ask. "We're considering taking it the next time."

"Oh, you must do it. We went to some recently discovered Hindu and Buddhist temples. We even saw a Sumatran tiger. There were gorgeous birds all around us. I took my sketch pad and had a great time."

"How did you hear about it?"

"My boyfriend recommended it. I felt terrible he couldn't go at the last minute. He woke up with this terrific headache. I was reluctant to go by myself, but he insisted, and I'm so glad he did. You should definitely go."

It sounds like she didn't know about the police interview yesterday. Or else she's a brilliant liar. My gut tells me she's on the up and up. I decide to take a chance.

"My name is Lexi—"

"Good morning. I believe you're in my seat," Javier says from directly behind me. Chills slither down my neck.

"I am so sorry. I was just asking about the jungle tour," I say and stand abruptly. To Karista, "Thank you. I believe we will take it. Sounds like fun."

I make my way back to our table to find Steve has arrived.

"I tried to catch your attention," Steve says.

"I was just about to tell her who we are. A minute longer and he would have heard me."

"Not good."

"Let's go upstairs and see if there's enough battery left to call the police," I say.

"If it isn't, maybe we can find a place to plug it in when they get the kitchen generator running."

#

Back in the room, I rummage through my bag. I was sure I put the phone in it.

Steve notices and shakes out the bedspread to see if it's just caught in the folds, but it's not there. He checks under the bed, I check under the cushions on the chair. It's not here.

"This isn't good." I double check the room safe. Our passports and cash, all okay.

But I notice my robe's not on the hook in the closet where I left it. I look through the closet more carefully. I finally locate the robe in the back corner, rolled up on the floor. Definitely not where I left it.

I step back and take a careful look around the room. The top dresser drawer is slightly crooked, one pillow on a chair is only partially zipped. My toiletries in the bathroom have been moved. Someone has searched my room and Steve's things in the living room.

Then it hits me. Andre's Glock is gone, too.

"Has to be Andre," Steve says. "He was the last one to leave our rooms last night."

"This was done while we were at breakfast. Andre's a

master. If he searched the room, we'd never know it. And what would he gain by taking the sat phone and his own gun? It doesn't make sense."

"I didn't see him at breakfast. He could have done it," Steve insists.

I decide not to mention that Andre was back later last night and slept in my room. He left for his own room right after the sun came up, long before Steve was awake.

I pause to think. "Javier came downstairs later to breakfast than Karista. I'll bet since he didn't find answers to whoever was on the third floor last night, he's searching all the guest rooms."

"That makes sense, but what's going to happen if he checks our outgoing calls and redials the bank?"

"Not good. He probably knows that Karista's money is there. We could be in real trouble. We need to get out of here immediately."

"Karista?"

"I'm going to tell her about Denise. Then we'll head to the airport. Clark will be here later. He can deal with everything else."

#

From the lounge, Steve and I can see Karista and Javier on the patio finishing their meal. We hurry to the registration desk to talk with Ifrah.

"Morning. Did you hear about the uproar last night?"

"Oh, yes," she replies. "One of the guests discovered

two thieves in an empty room on his floor, but they got away. Please don't be worried. It has never happened before. We are asking all guests to lock their doors tonight, and we've hired extra guards."

Hopefully we won't be here tonight.

"What time does the jeep leave for the airport?"

"No airport run today. Last night the rain washed out the roads in several places."

Not good news. That means no Clark from the airport, either. I glance out the window. More dark clouds on the horizon. There's definitely the threat of another storm soon.

"Maybe tomorrow," Ifrah continues. "If the flooding lowers. The monsoon is early this year. We close for the season next week."

"I'd like to put in a call to the United States. Is there any way to do that?"

"I'm so sorry. All the phones are out, too. The wires must be down."

"Does that include the Internet?"

"Yes. I can let you know when things are working. Don't worry, the kitchen has a small generator. There will be no interruptions to the meal service."

It's not the meals I'm worried about.

Javier passes through the lobby and heads upstairs. This may be our chance. Steve and I hustle onto the patio and sit down at Karista's table.

"Hi, Karista. I'm Lexi Winslow, from the Bank of Beverly Hills and this is Steve Harrison, who I believe you know," I say as I sit.

"It's been a few years," Steve says.

Karista goes quiet and studies Steve for a moment. "I'm so sorry I didn't recognize you. You're a lot taller than I remember. How's your dad?" She stands to give him a hug and sits back down. "Imagine meeting you so far from home. It's great to see you."

I cut in, "Actually, your dad is the reason we're here—"

"No, don't tell me. He sent you. He just can't stop meddling in my life." She stands.

"Please sit down. I need to tell you Denise is dead."

Karista sinks back onto the seat. "What?"

"It happened the day you left. We found her two days later."

Karista stares at her hands, I can tell she's rethinking the day. Tears roll down her face. "Poor Denise. What do you mean 'found her?'"

"Murder."

She's shocked.

"What happened between you before you left?" I ask.

"What do you mean?"

"It happened in her bedroom."

She tries to absorb the news. "At my house? Sherry? Is Sherry okay?"

Steve nods. "Nothing unusual happened before you left for the airport?"

"Denise and I had another argument about Javier. She

didn't want me going away with him," Karista pauses. "She's made her feelings about him quite clear, and I didn't want to hear it again. We got in a shouting match. I told her if she didn't like it, she could move out. I'd been thinking about asking her to anyway."

"What happened next?" I ask.

"Javier arrived a little later. He was furious when I told him the things Denise said. Then he carried my suitcase down to the car and we left for the airport."

"Denise was alive when you left?"

"Of course."

"And you and Javier went straight to the airport?" Steve asks.

"Yes."

"Was Denise dating anyone at the time?"

"She'd started dating someone new recently. But we weren't getting along, so I never asked about it."

Hmm. Maybe the police are right and it was Nate who killed her. Still, the closet, the knife, it feels too much like Javier. I'm not convinced.

"The police will be contacting you. In fact they came yesterday to speak with you. Did Javier mention that?" I say.

"No, but maybe he didn't want to upset me."

Steve jumps in. "Is that why he met them with a woman dressed in your clothes and pretending to be you?"

"That's impossible. You're lying."

"Listen Karista, I know fathers never realize their

daughters are capable of taking care of themselves, but there's more going on here. We think you're in serious danger. We need to get you out of Sumatra." I say.

"That's ridiculous," Karista says. "I'm perfectly fine. If anything happens, Javier will take care of me."

"Javier is the danger."

"What?"

"We think Javier is a psychopath and we think you're his next target," Steve says.

"Don't be ridiculous. Javier would never hurt me. He's the sweetest, most caring guy I ever met. He loves me."

She should have seen him last night when he burst into our room. He was ready to kill.

"Once he has your money," I point out, "you're only a liability to him. A disposable liability."

"Please. That's my father talking. He thinks everyone is after our money. Besides, Javier has his own money that he inherited. He doesn't need mine."

"Does he really have money or did he just tell you that?"

"I don't have to listen to your crazy lies. You can tell my father we're going to get married. He can't stop us."

"You may not believe it, but you're smart enough to know you have to consider it. Anyone with money does. Have you checked your accounts lately?"

Steve jumps in. "If you don't believe us, look in the closet of the room directly across the hall from you. There are two dead bodies there of people that worked for him. Is that enough proof? And in the room next to that one, there's suitcases left from stupid women like you he's already killed."

She blanches and stands. "I'll do just that and then I'll tell Javier about your terrible accusations. I'm sure he'll have something to say to you."

Not good. I'm sure he will.

"If you spread your ridiculous story, he'll sue you for slander. Is Denise really dead or is that a lie, too?"

"Karista, please don't—"

She stomps away and heads upstairs toward their rooms.

"Is she stupid or what?" Steve says.

"Knock it off, Steve. Victims of sweetheart scams aren't stupid. They're trusting and have no experience with con men. Come on, we don't want to be sitting here when Javier comes looking for us. Let's make ourselves scarce in the gardens for a while.

"If we're going, we should take our IDs and cash just in case. All our stuff is up in the room," Steve says.

"I don't think there's time."

"I'll be fast. Wait here."

"Steve, no—"

Too late, he's gone upstairs. Of all the crazy . . .

If Javier is smart, and he gives ample indication he is, the bodies and suitcases we saw on the third floor last night are already gone. He seems to have a free hand here and lots of support. He doesn't know what was seen or who we were. He can't risk that the police are on their way. As soon as Karista talks to him, he'll want to take us out.

Come on, Steve, hurry. It's not worth it.

I'm relieved when he hustles down the stairs.

"Javier and two of his men are in our rooms."

"Let's steal a jeep," I say. "It will get us at least as far as wherever the road is washed out. You can walk from there and find help. I'll come back in the jeep and keep an eye on Karista until you get back. They'll think I left with you. I can hide. A boat would be smarter, but we'd never make it down that long dock without a bullet in our backs."

"I'm not leaving you here alone."

"Steve, I don't know what else I can do. We need the police. Please don't argue." I don't mention my other motive, which is to get him safely away from here.

He doesn't like that plan at all.

I try not to think about Karista. I'll only be away an hour, I estimate. Javier will be afraid to hurt her if we can get away. All he has to do is continue the romance and deny everything when the police show up. Maybe if I think it enough, I'll believe it.

I could go to Andre, but who would he side with, Javier or us? That's too big a risk. I don't want to abandon Karista even for an hour, but what can I do? I'm being forced to choose between Steve and her. If only I was by myself, I could evade Javier and keep an eye on Karista, but I can't put Steve in danger. And I can't help either of them if I'm dead.

CHAPTER 22

Steve and I race down the hall to the door leading to the compound behind the hotel. When we reach it, we stop. I scan the area. There's no one in sight. We head for the garage.

I can see Andre over on the dock, but I try not to catch his eye. I think he sees me, but I duck out of sight. Pursuit won't be far behind us, we can't linger.

Steve and I slip into the garage. The two tour jeeps and an SUV are parked in the lot.

Three armed local men enter the compound from the hotel. They must work for Javier.

"That was fast," I say.

"What're we going to do?" Steve asks.

I think the sight of the armed men makes him realize this is not a game. We could die today.

I try to be reassuring. "We'll think of something. It's

possible their presence isn't related to us." Not that I believe it.

"They just happen to be carrying their weapons around a resort hotel for the fun of it? I don't think so. Maybe you've got a bomb in your pocket we can use?"

The three armed men move to the far side of the compound and light clove cigarettes. The scent drifts in our direction.

"Good idea. Wait here."

He gives me an alarmed look.

"Don't worry. I won't desert you."

I find a rear door to the garage and creep to the nearby storage shed. Time is not on our side. It won't be long before Javier shows up and he makes a thorough search of the hotel and the grounds for us. I head for the trash bins where the liquor and wine bottles are thrown out. I rummage through, grab four and head back via the storage shed where I score some matches.

Steve's freaking out by the time I rejoin him with the wine bottles. I give him the job of emptying the remaining liquid from them.

Searching the garage, I locate a partially filled can of gasoline and some rags near a lawnmower.

On my way back to Steve, I pass three sets of vehicle keys hanging on the wall inside the entrance. I slip the two for the jeeps into my pocket.

By the time I return to Steve, I can see he's even more anxious. "Ever make a Molotov cocktail?" I ask.

Some hope shows on his face. He listens to my instructions carefully as we turn the four bottles into grenades.

When we're finished, I check on the three men.

They've finished their smokes and are moving toward the garage.

I hand Steve the keys for the jeeps. "Can you drive stick and four wheel drive?" He nods. "Dad had an old Land Rover for years."

"When I throw the first one, run for the closest jeep, start it up, and take off. I'll try to create as much distraction as I can."

He looks at me in surprise. "Aren't you coming with me?"

"No matter how I try to rationalize it, I can't go without Karista."

"I'm not leaving you here."

"Don't make me choose between you and her. Just go. You may be our only hope for help. Try to get to the police."

"I'm staying. I can help."

I can tell he's serious. He might even be as stubborn as I am. I give up, we're wasting time. I need to get to Karista as soon as possible.

"Oh, no." Steve points.

It's Karista. She's here, in the compound right now. I watch her hug the shed wall and check out the area. I wave to get her attention and point to the guards. We watch as she spots them and ducks between the vehicles heading toward us. Looks like she changed her mind about staying here.

At the same moment she drops down, one of the armed men sees her. He aims his weapon and opens fire. Bam! Bam! Bam!

"Why are they shooting at her?" Steve asks.

"Javier must have decided Karista is a danger to him."

She drops flat on the ground, covering her head. Bullets tear through the vehicles. Gasoline pours out, spreading around them.

That's done it. Those jeeps aren't going anywhere. Javier's men are definitely here to stop us. They didn't even pause before they fired on Karista.

"Now," I say to Steve.

We light three bottles and hurl them at the two nearest men. The bottles explode before the men even register what they are. They go down from the concussion.

"Run," I yell at Karista as I race toward her.

Steve heaves the fourth bottle at the remaining man. The man stares in shock as it bounces harmlessly at his feet. It doesn't explode.

Karista and I are totally exposed. Smiling, the man raises his gun and carefully aims at us.

Steve yells, "Run."

Safety is too far. Karista and I freeze, caught in the man's sights.

He lingers, smiling as he aims.

Screaming, Steve charges at the man's back.

He spins to face Steve, but before Steve closes the distance—Ka-Bam! The dud bottle explodes.

The man disappears behind the smoke.

Steve is knocked backward.

I push Karista in the direction of the jungle. "Go. Run." Retrieving Steve, I support him as we stagger along following behind Karista.

Two more armed men round the corner of the hotel in time to see us.

Alarmed at the sight of their comrades lying on the ground, they fall back. It takes them a moment to regroup, but soon, they fire at our stumbling backs. Luckily, they're too late. We make the cover of the jungle.

I pause for breath and look back.

Attracted by the gunfire and explosions, Andre appears in the compound just in time to watch our flight. Just then Javier appears in the hotel doorway to the compound. He furiously signals his men to follow us.

We sprint deeper into the jungle.

CHAPTER 23

Running through the jungle is not easy. The undergrowth is dense and the ground marshy.

I pause when Steve pulls out the eight-inch curved knife he stole from the lobby wall yesterday. He uses it to help our progress. Sadly it's too short to be much help. A machete would be better. Better? What am I saying? Even the thought of a machete makes me shudder.

The storm seems to be closing in. There are rumbles of thunder in the distance. Just what we don't need.

We pause to catch our breath. "Thanks for messing up my escape. I could have been driving to Medan by now," Karista says.

"You were dead meat, sister," responds Steve. "And the roads are out."

It's clear from her expression that she didn't know that.

He continues, "We'd all be safe if you hadn't told your

boyfriend about us."

There's pain on Karista's face.

I cut in. "Keep your voices down. We better concentrate our energy on getting out of here."

Sounds of close pursuit reach us. I ask Karista, "You coming?"

"I don't need you. No way." She pulls out her cell phone and dials.

Steve and I disappear into the dense vines and foliage on the far side of the clearing as the sound of pursuit approaches.

A short way along, I stop. "Wait."

Looking back, I can barely make out Karista through the underbrush.

As the noise from the pursuers gets even closer, Karista looks around in indecision, then fear. Scared, she dashes into the jungle toward us.

"How long are we going to wait for her?" Steve asks.

"Get going. She's coming now."

Karista catches up with us. "Damn phone. There's no coverage"

Steve can't resist. "So why are you here? You don't need us."

"I thought about what you told me about those bodies, and I went to that room on our floor. There weren't any bodies in the closet." She pauses and takes a deep breath. "But there were some blood spots on the floor."

I glance worriedly behind her. "We better stop talking

and get moving."

I hustle them single file as fast as I can. Steve keeps hacking vines out of our way with the knife. After a few minutes, Karista grabs the knife from him and takes the lead to help out. She does a credible job with the knife. We move faster.

As I watch her back, my thoughts aren't good. I don't like this situation at all. We're not prepared to survive in the jungle. What if I can't get them home safely? The responsibility is overwhelming.

#

An hour later, dehydration and the oppressive humidity have drained our energy. We're covered in sweat and a gazillion bug bites that itch like mad. Thank goodness I put on long pants this morning, but Karista's not so lucky in her pretty capri pants. I can see the deep scratches and welts all over her calves and shins. Who knows what diseases we've acquired? We haven't run into any cousins of the reticulated python yet, although we've heard many unseen critters skitter away at our approach.

There's a sharp rat-a-tat-tat sound in the distance behind us.

"Was that lightning?" Asks Karista. She studies the dark clouds above.

"That was an automatic weapon."

"What are they firing at?" Steve asks.

"Thankfully, not us. Keep moving."

The dark clouds have thickened overhead. Rain would almost be a blessing at this point. We can't go much farther. I wipe the sweat out of my eyes. The salt from it really stings.

Then the jungle opens up a bit, making the going easier. If I never see another vine again I'll die happy, but soon the swampy ground makes walking even more difficult.

The wind increases and I glance up at the darkening sky. "Looks like the storm is almost here."

"It's a good time to stop and forage," Karista adds.

"I haven't heard the searchers for a long time. Do you think we've lost them?" Steve asks.

I shrug. "I doubt it. We're leaving a trail any tracker, even a bad one, could read like a highway. Maybe the storm will help cover our tracks. We'll have to stop soon anyway. It won't be safe to travel at night. Let's see if we can find a place to hole up."

Karista looks around. "We'll have to make a shelter."

I agree. I find a clear space between two trees located on slightly higher and dryer ground. "This will do. See if you can find something strong enough to hang as a support between the trees." She gets the idea immediately and starts looking around.

I set Steve to finding leaf-covered branches. Karista soon returns with a small fallen tree, roots and all. I like that she's pitching in. We manage to tie it horizontally in place between the two trees using vines.

Lightning cracks close by. As tired as we are, we move faster. With the cross-bar in place, we create a lean-to by adding Steve's and my tree branches and broad leaves from banana trees and other nearby foliage.

"Let's strap those down by weaving some vines through them," Karista suggests.

I admit it's an excellent suggestion and I'm impressed by how well she's adapting and helping. Not at all what I expected from a rich, spoiled Beverly Hills girl.

It's dark by the time we finish. Seconds later, the skies open up and rain pours through the jungle. We scramble for the lean-to.

Karista hastily rearranges some of the roof leaves to stop leaks. There's no chance of anything being dry enough to make a fire. We huddle together for body warmth.

The pounding rain blocks out all other sounds as we drift off to an uneasy sleep.

Our rest doesn't last long. In the middle of the night, the storm tears away our make shift roof. We huddle together as the down-pour continues.

CHAPTER 24

The noise of the jungle denizens wakes me before first light. Steve and Karista are still asleep. I guess we were too exhausted to stay awake in spite of being drenched.

The storm has passed for the moment, but there are still threatening clouds in the distance that don't look promising. I'm stiff, hungry, and soaking wet. There's not much chance that's going to change anytime soon.

After the rain started last night, I showed the kids how to use banana leaves to collect the rain water, but the storm was so fierce, the banana leaves are smashed and gone. I take my shirt off and squeeze the rain water out of it and into my mouth. Steve and Karista wake and do the same.

Unless it rains again, what comes out of the clothes we're wearing may be the closest thing we get to uncontaminated water all day.

"So what now?" Steve asks.

"I think we should head to the northwest. It will keep us out of the deeper marshes by the coast, and the highway is in that direction. With luck, maybe we can get a car to stop or find a house."

"All this is pretty wild territory isn't it? I read about four foot tall monkey men that are like Sumatra's version of big foot—" Steve says.

"You're afraid of 'little foot'?" Karista cuts in.

"Those are real, but supposedly very shy," I explain. "They're called Orang Pendeks."

"What about the lost tribes, and the leopards, and the poachers, and tigers?"

"I did see a tiger the other day," Karista contributes. She and Steve exchange a worried look.

"Do either of you have a better suggestion?" I say.

Steve says, "No, but—"

"Then that's what we'll do."

Karista sneers at Steve. "You really need to get out of the city more."

"Like you ever have?"

"My nanny loved the survival shows on television. You can learn a lot of stuff from them."

"Even I know those shows are all staged. The host always spends the night in a hotel. Not out in the wild like he says."

"If you had a choice, would you stay in a hotel or on an iceberg?"

"Well, that's pretty obvious," Steve says.

"See. A hotel would clearly be a better survival choice. I rest my case."

"Enough," I interrupt. "Let's get moving."

#

Twilight approaches after another long, grueling day. We've put a bit more distance between us and the hotel, but I wish we were able to travel faster. We came to some clearings, which forced us to circle around the edges to avoid being seen if our pursuers were close behind us. It doubled the time it would have taken to go straight across in the open.

In an effort to cool off, we didn't even bother to take off our clothes and took a quick duck into a stream we passed. Then let our clothes dry on our bodies as we moved on. The fierce humidity wouldn't let anything dry all the way. Sweat stinging our eyes and pouring down our bodies has become a constant. One good thing about the humidity is that it helps slow some of our fluid loss.

It drizzles on and off through the late afternoon. Now, overhead, the roiling clouds portend more rain soon.

We're looking for any form of shelter possible when Steve calls out, "What's that? Some rocks?"

Our eyes follow his pointed finger, then we hurry in that direction. As we get closer we find a huge vine-covered, stone statue of Buddha with an opening underneath it into a crawl space. There's no sign of anyone being here in the last hundred years or so. If we ever make it out of here, I'll report it to one of Sumatra's heritage groups.

"The tour guide said there were lost temples all over this area," Karista says.

We carefully search the cavity under the Buddha and remove some debris. Surprisingly, it's pretty clear. The space is about five feet tall and about six by ten feet wide with the opening on one of the six foot sides. We check it carefully for any slithering varmints.

The storm is closer now with occasional flashes of lightening. The wind picks up, and the temperature cools. The dank, primal smell of the jungle lessens with the air movement.

I quickly hunt for anything edible. I locate some small cassava roots but can't find anything else. Karista and Steve collect dry wood and grasses for a fire.

Karista calls out, "Hurry. I'm cold and I could eat a horse."

Steve says, "If there was a horse around here, something ate it already."

I turn over a log and find some big grubs. Perfect. I pass them to Steve for him to hang on to. "Bet you wish you were sitting in a cushy vice president's office right now."

"That's my parent's idea." He stops walking and looks at me. "Is that really what you think I'm about? All I ever wanted to do was be a fraud investigator. Okay? I admit it. I did insist Dad put me in security. I wanted to impress you with how smart I was. Impress my dad, too. Only I never counted on failing. I've made so many mistakes on this trip. And those bodies in the closet . . ."

He turns his head away.

"There's not much about this trip that has anything to do with our job," I tell him.

I widen my search to find more food. Turning over another log reveals more grubs.

Thunder rumbles closer.

I drop the grubs with Steve to add to the rest.

"Are we really going to eat these?"

"Yes. You know, I didn't get to thank you for what you did back at the compound. That guard would've killed us for sure."

"You would have done the same thing, just like you did in Toronto for that Canadian agent."

"How do you know about Toronto?"

"Are you kidding? We studied that wire transfer case in class. You're famous."

"Maybe once."

"Don't kid yourself. We learned about your money laundering case in Shanghai, the forged checks case in London—"

"And then there was Sydney." Bitterness creeps into my voice.

"Sydney? I never heard about Sydney."

I don't answer.

CHAPTER 25

The scary animal sounds I hear outside the Buddha let me know that things are definitely going bump in the night. It makes me thankful for our temporary shelter. There's also something reassuring about being under the literal protection of Buddha.

Steve, Karista, and I huddle around the dry tinder Karista collected.

"What's the point?" she asks. "I collected all this stuff and we have no way to start a fire."

I ask for her cell phone. I remove the lithium battery and put it under some of the dry grasses and twigs. Using a sharp rock, I jam it hard into the battery. When the released lithium hits the oxygen, there's a small spark. Enough to light up the grass and twigs.

"Wow," Steve says, impressed.

I am, too. "I heard about doing this, but this is the first

time I've tried it."

Before long, we're toasting the grubs on skewers made from a splintered piece of bamboo. The fire works perfectly because cracks in the rocks that form the base of the Buddha, as well as the opening, let the smoke escape safely.

Thank goodness we found some protection from the rain. The best thing is that the storm probably sent our pursuers hustling back to the hotel for the night.

Steve eyes the grubs unhappily. "I know people do this. I've seen it in movies and TV shows. Somehow it's harder when you have to do it yourself."

Karista also looks disgusted. I offer the first one to Steve. He's not about to admit he's as repulsed as she is. He manfully pulls a grub off the skewer, then screws up his courage and pops it in his mouth. He swallows without chewing. Probably a good option. I have to smother a laugh. This is the same guy who charged directly at an armed gunman yesterday.

"Hey," Steve says. "This isn't bad. He takes a second grub, giving Karista a superior look. "You should try them."

I take one and pop it into my mouth. I look down. Amazing. I've even managed to get some spots on my shirt from the grubs. Well, the joke is on the spots. For once, it doesn't matter.

I catch Steve watching me. "How'd you learn about this kind of stuff?" he asks.

"Boy Scouts," I say.

He sticks one in his mouth. He rolls it around tentatively and starts to chew.

"You mean Girl Scouts," Karista says.

"No. It was the Boy Scouts. The boys always had all the fun. Hiking, camping. Girls were stuck with cooking and sewing. Not my thing. My dad was the local boy scout leader, so I got to tag along on some of their outings."

No way is Karista going to look bad in front of Steve. She steels herself and casually tosses a grub into her mouth. And promptly chokes on it. Steve thumps her on her back, making the grub go down as she inhales sharply.

Not wanting to touch the knife, I ask Steve to cut and skewer some of the sliced cassava root. He gets fancy and alternates the roots with more grubs like a shish-kabob.

"You better eat some more," Steve says, holding a skewer out to Karista.

"He's right. We might not be so lucky tomorrow."

Karista doesn't respond. She appears deep in thought. Finally she says, "Denise's death is all my fault."

There's a loud snarl from a wild animal outside.

"What was that?" Karista says.

"Probably one of the big cats," I say.

"Will they come in here?"

"The fire will probably be enough to keep it away."

"Probably?"

"Well, hello." We jump as a sodden form fills the entrance. "Permission to enter?" Without waiting for an answer, Andre stumbles in. "I can't tell you how wonderful it was to see your fire.

I'm stupefied to see him, but something's wrong. "What on earth are you doing here?"

"I took a little stroll and ended up in the neighborhood." He warms his hands over the fire.

He must be really tired, because he's slurring his words badly.

"Are you hungry? Here have some of this." I pass him a skewer of grubs, but he waves me off.

Finding his voice, Steve demands, "Answer the question. What are you doing here? Is anyone with you?"

"I saw the shootout by the jeeps and followed you. I thought I could help. To my great shame, I seem to have been shot."

He has to be joking. "Why would anyone shoot you?"

"I was coming to your rescue."

"That's a nice change."

"You're a bad influence on me," he says. "After all these years and all the dodgy places I've been, this is the first time I was ever shot."

He moves his arm and I see the blood seeping from his shoulder. Alarmed, I reach for him, but I'm too late. He keels over on his side and passes out.

CHAPTER 26

I pull Andre's wet clothes away from his body to find a festering bullet wound in the fleshy part where his arm joins his shoulder. It's oozing blood. As I touch the area, he winces and groans in pain.

Karista and Steve watch nervously as I rip his shirt tail and use it to clean the area. I add pressure and the bleeding slowly dries to a trickle. That done, I feel the back of his shoulder. There's no exit wound. The bullet is still inside. Not good.

At least the bleeding has slowed, but the chances of infection are inevitable under these conditions.

A tear creeps down my cheek. I must be the dumbest woman in history. I'm devastated by the thought he might be dying. I ask myself whatever made him come after us. He hates the jungle. But I realize I already know the answer. He came after me.

Setting his head down carefully, I stare at his face. No matter what happened with the police and my fall from grace, I still love him. I've tried so hard to deny it, but it's been there since I first met him.

I turn to Steve and Karista. "Remember when we heard gunshots yesterday? That must have been when he was shot."

I make Andre as comfortable as I can and wave off Steve's questions. I have a lot to think about and decisions to make. It's a long time after the others fall asleep that I nod off.

#

The early morning noises wake me. Groggily, I sit up. Steve and Karista slumber on. The rain has stopped, and the sky looks to be clearing. Even though the fire died as we slept, being in an enclosed, heated area has dried our clothes and bodies.

I move to Andre. He seems to be sleeping naturally. That's good. But when I put my hand to his forehead, I can feel he has a fever. I hush Steve and Karista as they wake. Let Andre sleep as long as he can.

We slip quietly outside.

"We need to leave him and keep going," Steve says.

"I'm not leaving Andre here alone in that condition. He'll die."

"I don't think it's a good idea to split up," Karista says.

"I agree. There's safety in numbers," I say

"He'll slow us down," Steve argues.

"I'd be surprised if they're still hunting us." I say.

"They'll be after us all right. Javier is stubborn. He won't be happy until he catches us," Karista says bitterly.

There's a moment of silence as we consider what she said. From what we've seen of Javier, her words have a serious ring of truth. We should keep moving.

Talk about between a rock and a hard place. There's no way I want Steve and Karista heading on alone. I'm responsible for them. Yet I can't leave Andre here. He needs a doctor. If we try to take him with us, it could be weeks before we find the main road. There's no way he'll last that long. But for all of us to stay here is just courting capture, and I have no doubts about how that would end.

I can see the headline: "All hope ends for three Americans lost in the jungles of Sumatra. Search parties called off for lack of any discovery." Not that there will be any actual search parties. Andre won't even be reported missing. In reality, we'll all be in shallow graves somewhere, killed by Javier and his men. I hate to be morbid, but—

Steve interrupts my thoughts. "Lexi, turn around slowly."

When I do, I'm face-to-face with twelve Batak natives, staring at us. They're carrying spears and knives. Two of the men carry a small tapir hung on a pole between them.

"Are these guys cannibals?" Steve asks. Part of me wants to say yes and freak him out, but I control myself.

"Their ancestors were. I think these gentlemen are your average, garden variety poachers." I don't mention that could be just as serious. One thing poachers don't want is to be seen.

Andre was right. My life is a farce. My patron saints must be named Dumb and Dumber. I touch my silver cross necklace. If I ever needed divine intervention, it would be now.

The natives close in a threatening circle, surrounding us. Steve, Karista, and I stand back to back. So this is it.

They grab us. Karista and I struggle uselessly. I manage to take one down with a blow to the side of his head. The men pause and hiss at me. Not good.

Suddenly they push Karista and me away from them, knocking me roughly aside.

They turn their backs on us and surround Steve. I force my way back into the group to help him. There I find the man with the tallest headress fingering Steve's bright, albeit dirty, batik print shirt.

When he talks, I recognize some of his words. He's speaking a dialect of the Bahasa language I know. These aren't a group of poachers. Unless I miss my guess, they're a native Batak group living off the land with little or no contact with civilization.

I start talking, pleased to see the men are listening and appear able to understand me.

The head man says they crossed our trail and followed it out of curiosity. I ask if they've seen anyone else this morning. "They've seen signs of men who appeared to be searching for something," I tell Steve and Karista.

"Yeah, us," Steve says.

The head man interrupts me and points to Steve before making a demand. The men around him nod in serious agreement, but his request makes me smile. I think for a minute and decide to negotiate. It goes quickly and the head man agrees.

He leads us farther into the jungle. His men trail along behind.

"What's going on?" Steve asks nervously.

"Just hang on. We're okay."

We finally reach a river bank. Apparently, we'd been parallel to it for some time, but were far enough away that we weren't aware of it.

The natives lead us down the bank to two dugout canoes. They point at the smaller one. It's just a hollowed out log and doesn't look like it will ride very high in the water, but it will easily fit the four of us. Perfect.

I inspect the canoe and paddles. Then nod to the head man. We shake hands.

Karista and Steve give me alarmed looks. I hold my hand up to reassure them.

The natives cluster tightly around a panicked Steve and the chief again. When they part, the beaming headman steps through his men wearing Steve's dirty batik shirt.

Steve emerges shirtless and carrying a foot-long totem stick. He gives me a dirty look. "You could have warned me."

"Where's the fun in that?" I say.

Karista snickers. "I wish I had a camera."

I turn to thank the head man. The group has vanished, melting back into the jungle. A shiver runs up my back. Thank goodness they were friendly. This is definitely their world and not ours.

"Thank you for giving up your shirt."

"Like I had a choice? What now, Auntie?"

"Now we have a canoe and maybe a solution to our problem. This is the same river that empties into the bay next to the hotel. In our current situation, I think we should head back toward the hotel."

"No, that's too dangerous," cries Karista.

Steve grasps my idea. "They'll be hunting for us out here," he says, "They'd never dream we'd head back and end up behind them. Brilliant."

"But the canoe will sink if we try to take it out in the ocean. A wave would sink us. There's not enough freeboard," Karista says.

"True, but maybe the road is open now and we can steal a car or a boat and get to safety. The canoe is big enough to hold all of us, and Andre can travel in it easily. It's definitely the quickest route to medical treatment."

"That's a great plan," Karista says.

Before long, we've retrieve Andre and place him in the canoe.

"I thought you deserted me," he says.

"I wouldn't do that."

Before we take off, I check his wound. It's seeping, but the bleeding actually seems to be lessening. He looks stronger, too. We lay him down on the floor of the canoe. He's asleep instantly.

"How'd you ever get involved with a creep like him?" Steve asks.

"It wasn't exactly planned."

At this point, I feel it's only fair to answer his questions. "How much was in the HR report you read about my arrest?"

Karista listens, surprised.

"Practically nothing," Steve says.

"A couple years ago, I was sent to a cattle station outside Sydney where an Italian count named Orsini lived. I was there to check the books on the count's nephew's trust fund. As executor, the count claimed the huge losses in the trust fund were because of bad investments. It was a lie. The count had embezzled most of it, and the bank I worked for wanted to bring charges.

"At the same time, Andre was a guest of the countess. We met, and I fell for him. Hard."

"How romantic," Karista says. I shoot a look at her young face. I can see my feelings at the time reflected in her eyes. So full of hope. Too bad I have to shatter her illusions.

"It was later that I learned that the woman he really had his eye on was in a portrait by Rembrandt and owned by the countess. She was the great, great, whatever grandmother of the countess."

"Oh,," Karista says.

"Then one day, the Rembrandt was gone and so was Andre. Since we hadn't hidden our interest in each other, the count claimed I was an accessory to the theft. It was the perfect cover to discredit my report on the trust fund. The authorities lacked enough evidence, or any evidence, that would prove me guilty, but I couldn't prove I was innocent, either. The suspicions stuck and led to my arrest. The bank I worked for in New York fired me. They didn't even wait for the outcome. Even though the police released me, the damage was done. From then on, I was tainted goods."

"I knew he was no good. How could he let that happen to you?" Steve says.

Bless him for taking my side.

"I can hear you, you know," Andre says from his prone position in the bottom of the canoe. "And I tried very hard to help Lexi when I heard she was in trouble. I followed what happened, and I would have turned myself in if she was charged."

"I still lost my job and my reputation."

"I know. I never regretted anything more. I did make sure Howard hired you."

"What?" I had no idea.

"You know Howard?" Steve sounds surprised.

"Back when he was with the CIA, there was a bad

incident in Istanbul that wasn't going to end well for him. I got a warning to him, and he managed to get out in time. He's not a man to forget a favor."

I'm stunned. Andre had my back all this time? Can that be true?

"Believe me, Lexi. It didn't take much. He'd already heard of you. When I explained what happened and that you were innocent, he couldn't wait to hire you."

His voice drops off, and before I can respond, he's passed out again. I cradle his head.

I say to Steve, "I think Howard's input is going to be nil if we ever get home. Your father will be furious when he hears what's happened."

I'm lost in thought as we paddle along. The river has a slow current that helps us.

Above us the birds and monkeys keep up their chatter. We spot a small Sumatran rhino drinking from the river bank. He's startled as we pass and disappears instantly into the dense foliage. There's even an occasional crocodile sunning itself on the bank. I hate to admit it, but I'm missing Steve's guidebook descriptions.

Occasionally, a fish or something else jumps in the water. Small amphibians and snakes swim away at our approach. The bugs never let up, covering us with red welts. Even so, it would be a peaceful day if our mission wasn't so critical. Andre sleeps on through it all.

Still, my mind wanders as we paddle along. Maybe I'll buy a kayak when I get home. I like moving on the river.

It's so pleasant. That is, if I can afford one on a hamburger-flipping salary.

After paddling silently for what feels like hours, I finally break the silence. "Guess you'll be telling your dad what a mess I've made of this case?"

Steve stops paddling and wipes his sweat-filled eyes. "You must have a really low opinion of me. I wouldn't do that to you. Besides, who's made a bigger mess than I have?"

I do believe him. He's a good guy. Seems like he's pretty down. I make a guess and ask, "Still feeling bad about the French girl and the beggar?"

He nods. "And Denise. How can someone do that?"

"I think that's one of the big questions of all time. And no one has found an answer yet."

"I didn't even suspect Francoise was a thief."

"Don't beat yourself up over it. So far you've only had book learning. That kind of thing is street learning. Look. When you were in first grade could you do algebra?"

"Of course not." He's not sure where I'm going with this.

"Don't be so hard on yourself. It takes time to learn this job or any job. That's all. The only way to get better is to keep learning, and it never stops. Remember that the crooks are evolving, too. There's always a new con or a variation on an old one appearing."

Steve sits silently, thinking.

Karista says, "I owe you both an apology. If I'd

listened to my father, none of us would be here. It's all my fault you're put in this danger."

"Let's put the blame for all this where it belongs. On Javier."

She says in a low voice, "I was so sure he cared about me."

We float a bit farther.

"Think we could trade the canoe in for Vito's yacht when we get there?" Steve asks.

"I'll trade for anything that will get us down the coast to a town with a doctor."

Vito. He's something that's going to require some thought. "Do you think Vito knows what Javier is up to in his hotel?" I ask.

Steve shakes his head. "He'll be furious when he finds out."

"Will he?" I wonder. "I think Vito must be in on it."

"Why?" Karista asks.

"Because Javier has free run of the hotel and the staff. Vito wants money to buy back his family plantation and Javier must pay him well."

There's a moment of silence as we consider the implications.

"How much longer?" Steve asks.

"Can't be too far."

"This sure beats hiking through the jungle." He leans over to splash water on his face.

A huge crocodile—jaws wide open—surges out of the

water at Steve.

I manage to jerk him backward in the nick of time.

The croc's teeth snap on empty air.

The water is suddenly roiling with crocodiles. The shallow canoe tips dangerously. If this keeps up, we'll be in the water and crocodile food in seconds.

"Lie down. Quick. Hang on."

We stretch length-wise inside the canoe. It rocks wildly, almost turning over. I lay on top of Andre in an effort to hold him in position as best I can. Karista's foot jams into my side.

The massive crocodile leans into the canoe trying to reach me. My end of the canoe sinks under his weight, putting me half in and half out of the water. He twists his head, trying to get an angle to grab me. His fetid breath fills my nostrils.

Andre's arms lock around me. Steve kicks ineffectively at the croc's side. Karista smacks him with a paddle to no avail.

Desperate, I grab my paddle and jam it down his gaping throat. He slips back into the water, thrashing his head furiously, trying to dislodge it.

The other crocodiles flee from his writhing contortions. Their sudden departure causes waves that tip our canoe perilously.

"Paddle," I yell. "Paddle hard!"

Steve grabs the remaining paddle from Karista and manages to propel the canoe away from the teeming, frothing mass of reptiles.

CHAPTER 27

After our near miss encounter with the crocs, we're all pretty shaken. Talk about having all your eggs in one canoe. Screw buying kayaking lessons. There isn't enough money in the world to make me use one after today. There aren't crocodiles in California, but there definitely are sharks in the Pacific Ocean. Not the two-legged thieves I chase, but the kind with fins and sharp teeth and big appetites.

I tell Karista to move to the bow to watch the river for any signs of more trouble. That leaves Steve and me to trade our only paddle back and forth. The crocodiles splashed a lot of water into the boat, which we have no way to bail out. It makes the canoe even lower in the water and to be less responsive. I guess we could pull up on the bank and turn it over to empty it, but no one wants to take the time or the risk of running into more dangerous animals. It's a good thing we're going downstream or we'd be in real trouble.

Dusk is falling and we're desperate to reach the river's mouth before dark. Being caught for another night in the open or on the river bank is a bad option. I put my back into paddling when it's my turn. I notice Steve doing the same.

Andre's fever is rising at an alarming rate. I have his head on my lap to keep it and the wound in his shoulder above the water level inside the canoe. I can feel the heat from his body. He needs a doctor as soon as possible.

It seems like forever to me by the time we reach the bay. Thank goodness for no more incidents with crocodiles, although we did spot some on the river banks.

It's almost dark, but we all breathe a sigh of relief when we see an area just inside the mouth of the river that's clear enough for us to stop. We pull the canoe out of the water between the mangroves and a pile of tree trunks and branches washed up by the river.

Armed with the paddle, Karista nervously offers to wait with Andre while Steve and I reconnoiter the path to the hotel. I'm concerned about leaving them alone, but Andre is in no condition to fight or run if we encounter any trouble. Andre doesn't like it but doesn't have a better plan.

"I promise, we'll be back as soon as possible." The words make me nervous as they come out of my mouth. "If we're not back by dawn, or there's trouble, paddle into the bay, avoid the hotel and try to get a fisherman to help you."

Andre puts his hand on Steve's arm. "Make sure nothing happens to Lexi."

"I'll do my best."

Andre nods in response.

Annoyed, I say, "I don't need a babysitter." To which Andre raises an infuriating eyebrow.

Steve and I head off on foot in the direction of the hotel. We manage to find a foot path. It must be one used by the locals when they come to the river to fish. It leads us in a meandering route back to the hotel. Our goal is to find some sort of transportation that will take us back to civilization.

When we reach the edge of the jungle near the hotel, we watch for a few minutes. From the angle we're on, we can see the hotel is dark except for the patio. The compound area seems quiet. We gather our courage and make the three-hundred-yard dash across the open space to the compound's outer wall.

With each step I take, I expect to feel bullets ripping through my body. It's with great relief that I finally throw myself down beside the protection of the compound wall.

I gulp in air to refill my lungs. I must have been unconsciously holding my breath. After a few minutes, Steve and I peer over the wall and into the compound. In the poor light, we can just make out the charred remains of the vehicles that burned.

"I wonder how they explained gunfire and the vehicles

blowing up," Steve whispers.

"Not to mention the dead bodies."

Unfortunately, there are no new vehicles of any kind to be seen. That must mean the road is still closed. Not good. I was hoping that Clark, the FBI man, had managed to get through. My hopes for getting everyone home alive are dimming considerably. Well, if I'm going down, I'm going down fighting.

No cars means we'll need to steal a boat. It won't be easy with the area between the hotel and the bay devoid of any cover. The only way to the dock is above the marsh on the long wooden walkway that goes from the patio. The cover of darkness won't help because bright lights are strung the entire length of it. There'd be a high risk of being seen if we go that way.

We survey the hotel for signs of danger, but nothing appears different. We notice a few late diners on the patio. It looks like the power has been restored since the storm, or else a generator has been put to work.

Vito must be back. His yacht rides at anchor in the bay.

"I don't see any guards," Steve says as he looks longingly at the food on the patio. "Stay here a minute."

Before I can protest, he disappears into the garden. This is not a time to get separated.

I continue watching for signs of Javier or Vito. Neither is visible. I do notice a waiter set his tray of food on the edge of the patio while he refills coffee. When I look again, the tray is gone.

The waiter returns for it and seems confused. Where did it go? I duck as he scans the area.

A few minutes later, Steve rejoins me. And he's carrying the tray. He hands me one of the plates. My stomach does handsprings in happy anticipation.

We devour the food hungrily, eating half and putting the rest in our pockets for Karista and Andre. I feel much stronger with something in my stomach.

Fortified, we debate our next move.

"Maybe we could get into Vito's office and call or email for help?"

"I'd hate to get trapped inside the hotel. Wait a minute, wasn't there a phone in the garage?"

In a heartbeat, I'm over the wall and racing for the garage with Steve right on my heels. Even in the dark, we manage to find it on the back wall. I grab the receiver in anticipation. After a second, I slam it down on its hook. The phones still aren't working.

"It's only a staff intercom. It goes to the reception desk. There's no way to get an outside line from here. I hope no one noticed I picked it up. Let's move out of the compound in case someone comes looking."

We head quickly back to the wall and scramble over it.

"I forgot, even if we did get to a phone, we'd still have to go through the switchboard to get an outside line. Andre needs help as soon as possible."

"Yeah, we need to let people know what's really going on here."

"The guests are too big a risk. Who knows what they've been told about us. They may just turn us over to Javier. Let's head back to the canoe. We can paddle into the bay and steal one of the fishing boats now that it's dark."

We do the three-hundred-yard dash across the open area and back to the jungle path. This time, I don't hold my breath. Once on the path, we slow to a cautious walk. It's totally black. Any ambient light is blocked by the foliage. We have to feel our way along the path. It's not too difficult. The minute you make a mistake, you'll run into a wall of vines and other jungle plants.

I estimate we're about halfway back to the river. I'm pretending there will be no critters on the path when I notice moving lights up ahead. Flashlights! I grab Steve and shove him off the path and into the jungle. When we're safely hidden, we crouch down. Hopefully we won't be caught in the lights. Or by any critters.

The lights come closer. Their beams penetrate everywhere as they swing back and forth. The sound of men's voices can be heard. Finally, they're close. By the light from their flashlights, I can see two of Javier's armed guards moving on the path. The really bad news is behind them is a silent Andre, supported by Karista. Following them are two more guards with their weapons trained on them.

I can't believe the guards found them so fast. How did that happen?

"We have to stop them," whispers Steve. He starts to jump up.

I yank him back down. "There's too many. We can't help if we're dead. Our only hope is they don't know we're here." At least, I hope they don't.

Once they pass, we follow at a discrete distance. When they reach the hotel, I can see Javier alone at the head of the dock. He waves the guards toward the yacht.

Karista yells, "Help. Help." One of the guards jabs his gun butt into her stomach. She doubles over, going down and taking Andre with her.

The guards force them to their feet and hustle Andre and Karista down the walkway toward the dock. My heart bleeds as I watch them stagger along helplessly. There's no doubt that their futures will be short if we can't rescue them.

"Bastards," whispers Steve. "I wonder where Vito is. We need his help."

"I'm sure he's around somewhere close, but I wouldn't look for help from him."

"Why? He's not going to be happy Javier's using his yacht."

"Think about that," I say. "Why would Javier do that?"

We watch in silence as Andre and Karista are loaded roughly into the dinghy. The dinghy delivers them to Vito's yacht in short order. Karista struggles as she steps out onto the swim deck, but the guards roughly hurry her inside and out of sight. The other guards haul Andre onto the deck. He can barely stand. They shove him along behind Karista, until they, too, disappear into the ship's interior. The door shuts behind them.

CHAPTER 28

"Swim out to the yacht? Are you crazy?"

Steve's right. I'm not thinking straight. If the crocodiles don't get us, the sharks in the bay surely will. The canoe is our only answer. We stumble as fast as we dare in the dark as we hurry back along the twisty path to the river. This time I'm so mad the critters better look out for me.

When we arrive at the place where we left the canoe, I can barely see it in the dark. It's submerged half in and half out of the water. Steve grabs one end and I wade into the river to get to the other end. It takes all our strength before we manage to flip it over and empty out the water.

I groan. There's a huge hole smashed in the bottom of the canoe. The guards made sure it would never be used again.

I drop my end and return to the bank. I let myself sink

onto the ground. Steve looks at me hopelessly. He doesn't even have to say the words, what now?

Time and circumstance are not on our side.

My eyes work their way around the area. I have an idea, but the darkness makes it almost impossible to see. "Maybe we could lash some of the washed up logs from that debris pile to the canoe," I suggest.

"Worth a try."

We hasten to the pile to check it out and manage to roll and drag out two tree trunks about eight feet long. Steve uses his knife to cut lengths of nearby vines. We use those to lash a trunk to each side of the canoe. After that, Steve cuts branches to add to the canoe and logs as camouflage for the canoe and us. I weave them securely, make that as securely as possible.

Steve says, "Look what I found." He waves our paddle above his head. "They tossed it over here."

What a relief. Our makeshift canoe won't work if we can't steer it. Next, we have to push it into the water. Not an easy task with the logs' roots digging into the dirt. It's fortunate we only have to go a couple yards.

Steve lets out a muffled cheer when it actually floats. I notice the vines we used to tie the logs to the canoe are coming loose already as the logs settle in the water and the branches shift. Not good, but the whole contraption only has to hold together until we reach the yacht. No point dwelling on what happens after that. We'll have to play it by ear. It's our only option.

We darken our faces and visible skin areas with mud, commando fashion and scramble on board. Steve uses the real paddle, and I use a piece of wood from the debris pile as a second one.

The moon's obscured by clouds, which provides us with good cover. I just hope we're not too late. If Vito headed his yacht out to sea right away, it will be long gone by the time we reach the bay. We don't even know if Karista and Andre are still on board. It seems like forever since we watched them march down to the dinghy.

Finally, we float out of the river's mouth into the bay.

I'm relieved to see the yacht still at its mooring place.

We silently paddle, while lying low and trying not to let the paddles be visible or make any noise.

As we get closer, we spot a guard making rounds. He pauses for a smoke on the level above the swim deck. Thank goodness they left the swim deck down. We'd need grappling irons or ladders to board the ship if they hadn't.

We float silently closer and soon we're directly below the bow. I grab the anchor chain to keep our makeshift canoe from floating on past. We can hear the guard pass above and head toward the bow. We wait quietly. The water laps against the side of hull.

The faint sound of talking carries across the water from the hotel. It's hard to believe that we're out here fighting for our lives, and the people inside are totally oblivious to our situation. It's a lonely feeling.

We pause until the guard moves by for the second

time. I let the canoe noiselessly drift back to the swim deck, taking special care not to let it bump against the hull. We tuck in beside the dinghy and wait tensely for the guard to pass again.

I have no plan other than to find Karista and Andre and try to get them away. I can only hope they're okay. We don't even know how many people are on the yacht. I figure our chance of success at less than 10 percent if I'm being honest.

There aren't any illusions about our fate if we're caught. These people have proven that they think nothing of cold-blooded murder. I just wish Steve wasn't here. He's a good kid and doesn't deserve to be in a situation like this. I tried to talk him into staying behind before we left and raising a stink with the guests if I don't return. He wouldn't have any of it. He's not short on courage, either.

We hear the guard pass and hold our breath, afraid he'll glance our way and notice us. To our relief, he passes without stopping.

I signal the "go ahead" to Steve by waving. He clambers silently onto the swim deck and ducks under the overhang of the upper deck. From there, he blends into the dark shadows, and out of sight. I follow him after I push the canoe as far away from the yacht as I can. If anyone sees it, hopefully they'll think its nothing of interest. I dart after Steve under the overhang and into the shadows.

We wait to hear if there's any outcry. My heart pounds so loudly, you'd think it could be heard in outer space.

The boat rocks slightly, we can still hear music coming faintly from the hotel. Nearby, a fish jumps in the water. As our ears attune, we can hear the murmur of voices inside the yacht.

As the guard crosses the upper deck, he pauses. We wait nervously for him to move on. We hear his footsteps go by. I breathe a sigh of relief, but it's premature. He approaches the nearby stairs and slowly descends to the swim deck. We brace ourselves. He draws even with our hiding place and stops to study our wet footprints across the deck.

Afraid to wait any longer, I slip behind him and take him down with my best karate chop. Steve hands me the guard's gun. I slam the butt into his head. The blow stuns him. He's out for the count. Steve and I catch him before he falls and drag him out of sight.

Steve uses his belt to fasten the guard's hands. I rip off a piece of the guard's shirt and shove it in his mouth. Steve uses the guard's own belt to bind his feet. Finished, we look at each other with new appreciation and, totally inappropriately, smile. We make a pretty good team.

Steve picks up the guard's gun and passes it to me. I give him thumbs up. Smart move.

Armed with one gun for me and Steve's antique knife, we cautiously descend into the interior of the yacht.

Unchallenged, we continue down the main passageway, finally pausing at the door to the small lounge where we hear voices. I note the voices are all male. None are Andre's and there's no clue regarding Karista. It's good we have some idea of the layout from our dinner with Vito.

I signal to Steve to go to the next door. I put my ear against it. There are sounds from inside. I turn the handle carefully. The door opens on an empty crew cabin. I close it and move on.

The following room is fitted with the latest high-grade color copier and other top-grade counterfeiting equipment. It's a small room, but set up efficiently. Boxes of passports from a multitude of countries, both real and forged, are piled on the counter. There are shelves containing inks, stamps, and credit card blanks. Stacks of real credit cards are strewn carelessly about. There's even a camera setup and backdrop to shoot passport pictures.

How brilliant is it to hide a counterfeiting workroom on a yacht? Who would guess? When you're ready, you can just motor over to Thailand or Malaysia and sell the fake documents. And if there are any problems, you can put out to sea and dispose of any evidence over the side before the police can catch up.

Vito and Javier must be in this together.

Steve and I back out and cross over to the next door. I hesitate before opening it, but there's no sound from within. There's no change in the murmur of voices coming from the lounge. Opening these doors feels like playing Russian roulette. Sooner or later, one is going to have something I don't like inside. I turn the knob cautiously.

Karista's there, tied against one of the crew's bunk

beds. She looks up, startled. Then recognizes us. I forgot our mud covered faces. I put my finger to my lips, cautioning her to be quiet. Steve steps in and cuts her bonds. From inside the room, I watch the passageway from a crack in the door. All is quiet. Steve and Karista join me there.

"Are you okay?" I whisper to Karista. She nods weakly. Steve puts his arm around her for support.

"Do you know where Andre is?"

She shakes her head. "They shoved me in here and took him away."

"Steve, take Karista out to the dinghy, don't start the motor, but untie it and push away form the yacht. Be ready to go if you see Andre and me. If you don't see us in a few minutes, take off and head south to the next town and get the police. Don't look back, don't wait. Don't try to come back in and save us. Promise me. Get Karista out of here."

He nods, not liking it.

We step out into the passageway in single file with Steve, then Karista, and me last with the gun. As we approach the door to the small lounge, we can still hear noises inside.

Suddenly, the lounge door swings open and Javier stands in the doorway.

"What—" He steps into the passageway, blocking it. There's a moment of shock as we see each other.

We're trapped. Javier is between us and the outside. I'm stuck behind Karista and Steve. I can't bring the gun

227

into play quickly enough in the narrow passageway without taking the chance of hitting either of them.

"Guards!" Javier yells, before ducking back into the lounge and slamming the door. We race past, climbing the stairs and emerging onto the swim deck.

Too late. Sajuk and the guards swarm the deck, their weapons all aimed at us. We've nowhere to go.

Still I have to try. I drop my gun and raise my hands in the air. When the guards relax slightly, I charge straight at Sajuk. We exchange a flurry of pounding blows until he lands a powerful hit to my midsection. It's over quickly. With the wind knocked out of me, I sink to the deck. I can't resist as Sajuk grabs me and lifts me to my feet.

Angry, the guards force us at gunpoint back down the passageway.

CHAPTER 29

Javier opens the lounge door with a smirk. "Bring our guests in, Sajuk."

To us, he adds, "So you survived the jungle. You may wish you hadn't."

The first thing I notice are identity papers and a passport with Andre's picture in front of Vito on his desk. Beside them are Andre's Glock and our satellite phone. There's not much pleasure in knowing I was right. Javier took them.

Then I see Andre tied to a chair. I let out a sigh of immense relief to find him alive. He's bruised, bloody, and barely conscious, but he's breathing. Even so, I can tell he isn't happy to see us, nor the condition I'm in.

He gives Steve a disapproving look. Steve can't meet his eyes.

"Et tu, Lexi? What does a guy have to do to make you

go away?" he manages.

"Stop trying to hog all the fun for yourself," I respond as our eyes exchange a mixture of love and sadness.

"The mud is a nice touch. It brings out the color of your eyes."

Javier cuts in, "This saves us some time. I was asking Andre about your whereabouts, and he wasn't being very forthcoming."

Vito watches silently from his desk as we're shoved against the wall.

Javier stands aside as Sajuk ties our hands in front of us. Sajuk pushes us roughly to the floor and then moves to a position nearby.

Vito looks at us with contempt. "You won't get away again."

"We need to get rid of them," Javier says.

"You bastard," Karista blurts at him.

"I didn't notice you complaining."

"Murderer. You killed Denise. You did it when you went back inside to get your keys, didn't you? I wondered why it took you so long."

So she remembered he went back into the house alone.

She spits at him, hitting his hand. He wipes it disgustedly on his pants and then backhands her across the face. "Bitch."

Steve kicks at him, catching Javier's knee. He receives a vicious blow in return, which catches him on the side, knocking him over.

"Denise got what she deserved. Nobody stands in my way."

Just because she got in his way? I can't believe how callous that is.

"You psychopath," Karista says. I totally agree.

Javier lifts his hand to strike her again.

"Enough," Vito intercedes. "They won't trouble us for long. We'll dispose of those three tonight and Karista after her father wires the ransom."

Javier interrupts, "No, Pai."

Pai? That's Dad in Portuguese. I sure didn't see that coming, but in hindsight it makes perfect sense. No wonder Javier has the complete run of the hotel including special service from the staff and waiters.

He goes on, "I'm done. I'm thirty years old. How long do you expect me to suck up to all these ridiculous rich women? I've been doing this since I was sixteen for you. Do you have any idea how demeaning it is? To hang on their petty words like they matter." He stares at Karista.

Her face goes white.

Vito cuts in, "You'll do what I tell you, Javier. You can't quit."

"Why? Because you want to buy some stupid plantation? Sell this yacht, the Goya, the hotel, or both. You have money."

Andre's eyes flicker open as he listens.

"That should give you more than enough. Plus whatever is in the cofre room," Javier continues.

Cofre? That's Portuguese for a safe. I can sense Andre's interest from here.

"Sell the Goya? Have you no pride? It's meant to be passed from father to son," Vito says.

"It's a remembrance from a family that disowned us. Pride and five dollars will buy you a beer," Javier says.

"It's part of your rightful heritage, like the plantation."

"People don't care about who your family is anymore. I'm moving to Bangkok when we're done with this." Javier waves his arm indicating us. "It's time I went out on my own. You have your fake documents to sell, the hotel, this yacht. What do you give me to live on? Pocket change."

"You're not going anywhere." Vito points at Karista, "We can get a lot of money for her."

"And a lot of trouble. I want no part of it. Already we've got these outside people involved. Use your head, Pai. It's time to lay low for a while. Cut our losses. No ransom is worth the risk."

Vito turns to us. "Yes, why are they involved? I think we need to find out."

Andre mumbles, "If it's money you want, I can pay my own ransom."

They look in his direction as he struggles to talk.

"You know Bernardo vouched for me when you agreed to do my documents. Call him. He can arrange it. My only involvement here is thinking she's attractive." He nods in my direction. "I have no quarrel with you. You know I won't be going to the police. Besides, I have friends like Bernardo who know where I am. If I disappear or am killed while dealing with you, word will get around that you're too dangerous to buy from. Your black market identity business will dry up quickly."

Vito looks thoughtful. "How much?"

"I can probably match whatever you're asking for her," he says, nodding toward Karista.

Vito hesitates.

My heart sinks. I can't believe how calmly Andre dismisses our lives.

Javier lounges beside the door, playing with a knife, exactly like the one Denise was killed with. "Really, Pai, does it matter?"

"I'll talk to Bernardo." Vito nods to Sajuk, "Bring him," and leaves.

Sajuk cuts the ties binding Andre. He can barely stand and stumbles as he follows Vito out. There's blood oozing between the fingers he's pressing against his wound, but I have to close my eyes. I can't believe I care about this man, and now he's walking away and leaving me all over again. How could I have been so stupid? I knew what he is. I should have left him in the jungle to his own devices and kept heading north. The kids and I are headed for a watery grave soon, and I have no way to stop it. Both Karista and I have been betrayed by the men we loved.

"Bastard," murmurs Steve as Andre passes.

Javier gives him a halfhearted kick. "No talking." He

settles back against the door and watches us, still toying with his knife.

Half an hour later, Vito returns. Andre lurches in behind him. Vito shoves the fake identity documents on his desk that he prepared for Andre into an envelope. He slides it toward him. "One of my men will run you to the dock. The roads should be open by tomorrow and you can leave then."

Andre nods, picking up the envelope with shaking hands.

"Herr Mueller is a guest and a doctor. Ask him to take care of that wound. Say it was an accident," Vito adds.

Vito's father, Alfonso enters. He pauses as he takes in the scene. "What's going on here?"

"None of your concern, old man. The dingy is headed for shore. Go with it."

Alfonso moves toward me with alarm. "These people are our guests."

"Perhaps you'd like to join them."

"Careful, Alfonso. Vito's going to kill us to cover the murders he and Javier have already committed," I say.

He turns to Vito in shock. "Murders? Is that right?" He reads the truth in Vito's face.

"Kidnapping, too," I add.

"This is what you've become?" asks Alfonso.

Vito backhands Alfonso. It seems Vito and Javier have perfected that move. Like son, like father.

While all eyes focus on Vito and Alfonso, Andre kicks

something toward me. I feel it hit my leg. It's a knife. I only have seconds to pull it out of sight, but I hesitate. A knife? I tell myself either I grab it and use it or we could all die. Logic and emotion battle inside me. My brain says to reach for it. I do, but my fingers won't touch it.

I finally force myself to grab it, but my hands shake badly. Use the knife or die, use the knife or die, I tell myself over and over. I can't believe I'm hesitating.

I cut the rope and slide the knife quickly to Steve. His eyes widen as he sees it. In a flash he frees himself. He leans over and cuts Karista loose.

I feel joy spread through me. Andre didn't abandon us. He's trying to get us all out of here.

With everyone still watching Vito and Alfonso argue, no one notices what we've done. I indicate to Karista and Steve to stay put.

"Shut up, old man. How else could I regain the heritage you lost?" He pushes Alfonso toward the door.

"What heritage will you pass on? I only lost a plantation. You've lost your honor."

Vito waves at Sajuk. "Get him out of here." He points to Andre, "Him, too."

Sajuk shoves Alfonso and Andre out the door to the passageway and into the arms of two guards.

"Lovely doing business with you, Vito," Andre says over his shoulder.

Sajuk shuts the door behind them and stays in the room.

Vito puts Andre's Glock to my head. "What brought you here?"

Sajuk turns his back on Steve and Karista to watch. "It was easy. Javier isn't too bright and he has expensive tastes." I figure it won't hurt to fuel the conflict.

Vito scowls at Javier. "So this is your doing?"

"No way."

"Come on, Javier. You killed Karista's roommate. The trail from Karista's credit cards lead straight to your hotel. You know the US police already sent the local police here once to question you. You won't be going back to the US for a long time unless it's in handcuffs. Or to any country with extradition to the US."

Vito turns on Javier, lowering the gun. "Americans are our best targets—"

I throw my ropes off as I leap to my feet and hit Vito as hard as I can with an uppercut to the chin. Sadly, the Glock falls beyond my reach. Vito and I scramble for it as Javier and Sajuk move toward me.

Steve scrambles to his feet and intercepts Javier with a surprisingly good kidney punch. Karista shoves her foot out, tripping Sajuk. In seconds it's a free for all. Only the odds are against us and losing will mean death.

Javier grabs me from behind, throwing me off balance, but I shake him away. He crouches, ready to bring his knife into play. We circle each other warily. Javier lunges at me knife first. I manage to dodge him, then twist to deliver a powerful kidney punch. He falls heavily and bangs his head on the corner of the desk with a sickening thud.

Bam! Unable to get a clear shot, Vito fires the Glock at the ceiling.

"Stop or Sajuk will break your friend's neck."

Sajuk has Steve in a headlock. He flexes his arm, showing how easy it will be for him to snap his neck. Pain crosses Steve's face.

I raise my hands. Sajuk releases him, letting him drop to the floor.

I duck and roll into Sajuk, catching him off guard. Then I leap up and jump kick him hard with both feet.

It doesn't faze him. He sways on his feet as if my blow were a summer breeze.

I back away, putting a table between us. A tank would be better, but there isn't one here.

Vito recovers from his surprise and aims the gun at me, but Sajuk stands between us. He can't get a clear shot. He concentrates, waiting for an opening. I struggle to keep Sajuk between us.

Sajuk finally manages to corner me in the tight quarters. He grabs me, squeezing my chest painfully.

"Kill her!" screams Vito. "Kill her!"

Sajuk smiles. He increases the pressure.

Vito drops on his knees next to Javier whose blood gushes from the wound in his head.

Javier seems mesmerized by the sight of the blood dripping down his face.

"Look," he whispers, "So much . . ." His eyes close. He's gone.

"Javier, don't die. I'll get help." Vito pleads. Steve and Karista freeze, horrified.

Sajuk, furious, squeezes me harder. "Ahhhhhh," I cry out in agony.

Steve realizes we're still in danger. He seizes a lamp from the desk and smashes it into the side of Vito's head. As Vito goes down, the Glock drops from his limp fingers.

Seeing his boss fall, Sajuk tosses me aside and, in a rage, starts for Steve.

Steve tries to back away but Sajuk doesn't even pause. He headbutts Steve, hard. Steve clings to the wall in an effort to stay upright.

I reach for the gun Vito dropped. As Sajuk moves in on Steve, my hand closes on the gun. I roll and fire at Sajuk.

Clutching his chest, he falls—dead.

All motion in the room stops. In the second of silence, I hear the putt, putt of the dinghy as it heads for the hotel, carrying Andre and Alfonzo away.

The passageway door slams open. We brace for a confrontation with the guards, but it's Andre who enters with one of the guard's weapons. He sways on his feet momentarily as his eyes quickly take in the situation. He turns to me and smiles weakly. "Why didn't you wait for me?"

When he takes me in his arms, I rest against him weakly. I know this is my safe haven. The place I long to

238

be.

After a moment, I realize that I can feel his heart racing hard. His body is hot, really hot.

Before I can react, Andre sinks through my arms and slides, unconscious, to the floor.

I really wish he'd stop doing that.

CHAPTER 30

I find the ship's first-aid kit and clean Andre's wound while Steve and Karista tie Vito to a chair with duct tape from the supply room. Steve finishes with a strip across Vito's mouth.

"Anything we can do?" he asks me.

I shake my head no.

He indicates Andre. "He's starting to grow on me."

He and Karista head up on deck.

I'm relieved when Andre regains consciousness. His high temperature scares me. I wish the dinghy would return.

I ask him, "What happened to all the guards?"

"Alfonso knew where Vito kept his guns. We got the drop on the guards, forced them into the crew quarters, and wedged the door shut. Then Alfonso went to get help and call the police. He'll be back soon."

Alfonso's idea of shortly doesn't match mine. The sooner Andre gets to Dr. Mueller, the better.

"I don't know how, but we should get you away from here before the police arrive."

"The police will start searching for me immediately. There's not enough time to get on a plane before they alert the airports and the ports. I don't have the strength to evade them anyway."

He is weak. Someone would have to travel with him. The thought of Andre in a Sumatran prison horrifies me. In fact, in any prison. "There has to be something we can do."

My eyes fall on the envelope of identity documents Andre received from Vito. They give me an idea.

Steve and Karista burst into the room. "Come. You've got to see what we found!" they say in unison.

Steve and I support Andre. Moments later, the four of us stare into Vito's cofre room, stunned. It's like discovering a pirate's treasure trove. There's heaps of cash, and gold, and jewels. I guess Vito doesn't believe in banks, but to be fair, I don't think there's any bank box in the world big enough to hold it all.

Steve playfully runs his fingers through the cash. He throws a fist full of bills at Karista. She laughingly throws some back. Like confetti, the air fills with currency from dozens of countries.

"It's too bad we have to turn it all over to the authorities," I say.

Andre gets a strange look on his face.

Steve and Karista continue their ruckus over the money as I slip away unnoticed.

Back in Vito's office, I grab our sat phone and head up on deck alone. At the railing, I stare out to the starlit sea. My fingers rub my silver cross. Off to the side, I can see the lights from the hotel patio. There's no sign of Alfonso's return yet. Andre wandered off saying he was going to lie down until Alfonso gets here since there's nothing we can do until he does.

Using the sat phone, I ask the operator to put me through to the police in Medan. After a few transfers, I finally reach the head of the department. I explain there's been trouble at the hotel and can they send someone. Immediately, he responds, but it will have to be by boat as the roads won't be open until tomorrow. I end the call when he starts asking me for specifics.

I better go check on Andre. He must be feeling pretty badly.

Just then, Andre descends the stairs carrying a canvas tote bag. He clutches the handrail for support, then staggers over beside me.

"You should be in bed."

He kisses me on the back of the neck as he braces himself against the rail for support.

"You were marvelous tonight," he says as his lips tease my ear. "If I'd only known that getting shot would bring us together, I would have done it sooner."

I turn in his arms. "I thought you weren't coming

back."

"I would never leave you in danger."

"Thank you."

We kiss passionately. I break off the embrace to search Andre's face. For a moment, the desire we feel for each other hangs between us. Then, like a magnet, Andre pulls me hard against him and we kiss again. Longer and deeper.

"I love you," he says in a low voice, his breath tickling my hair.

"Your definition of the word isn't the same as mine."

"I've never lied to you."

"True, but you did neglect to tell me a few things. Like when you told me you sold art for a living, you neglected to mention that the owners didn't exactly give you permission."

"Possession is nine-tenths of the law."

I give him a look. How can I be in love with him? A man I'll never be able to trust? If I can't even control my heart, what does that say about me?

"I was afraid I would lose you. How could I let that happen?" He continues after a moment. "I'm sorry about what happened in Sydney. I wasn't prepared to fall in love. You were the last thing I ever expected. Regrettably, my backers at the time were not the kind of people who accept failure. I had to choose. It would have been my life if I hadn't taken the Rembrandt back to Holland."

Can I believe him? I want to with all my being, but he's a man who represents my polar opposite. How can I tell his lies from the truth when the lies float so easily off his tongue?

"Come with me now. We could be such a great team."

"I won't play Bonnie to your Clyde."

"They lived life to the fullest."

"It didn't end well for them."

His kisses put a stop to any thinking. His hands move over my body. They feel like heaven. His touch is so light, so knowing, even though he can barely stand..

"Our relationship will never work," I whisper.

He holds me even closer. If only we could just ignore the world and be together.

After a few minutes, Andre says, "Then let's start over. Hi, I'm Andre. I steal things, but I've never hurt anyone. Well, not anyone who didn't deserve it."

"Since we're just meeting, please remove your hand from my butt." He does.

"Come on, play the game."

"Nice to meet you. I'm Lexi. I try to protect people from thieves like you."

He frowns. That's obviously not the way he hoped this would go. He starts again, "I'm Andre. I enjoy skiing, fine wine, fast cars, and fast . . . horses."

"All of which you pay for with other peoples' money."

"I was poor once. I didn't like it."

Impasse.

"Does it count that I dearly love you?"

Okay, he got me with that one. I don't know how to

respond, and when he kisses me again, my will turns to mush. I have no defenses against this man.

"I love you, too," I respond.

Across the bay at the hotel, the putt, putt sound of the dingy starts up and grows louder.

CHAPTER 31

When we arrive back at the hotel, we find Alfonso has already alerted Dr. Mueller, who meets us in my room. He's a short, plump, cheerful man with efficient hands.

I hold a flashlight as he works on Andre's wound, he constantly makes "Tsk, tsk," sounds. With professional aplomb, he cleans Andre's wound, stitches it, and declares he'll make a full recovery.

He follows his diagnosis with a round of shots for infection and a lecture about being careful handling guns. I don't know what Alfonso told him, but he'll know the truth soon enough when the police get here.

After Mueller finishes and leaves, Andre slips into his bathroom to clean up, taking the canvas tote bag he's been carrying since we left the yacht with him. At least the plumbing works.

I'd like to shower and put on clean clothes before the

police arrive, but my body is too tired to move. I sink into a soft chair.

Facing yet another police interrogation is not an encounter I'm looking forward to. All I need is another bad mark on my reputation or, worse yet, imprisonment. My eyes close.

#

I feel as if my eyes just closed when Andre shakes me awake.

"Come on. Wake up. The police just arrived at the dock. They want everyone downstairs." He's fully dressed in clean clothes with a clean jacket on, but he still looks weak.

Downstairs, we find the lobby lit with candles. The police are rounding up the guests and staff and herding us into the lobby. Then they escort the guests, one by one, down the hall and into Vito's office to be interviewed. Most return after a short period, but they're not allowed to speak with those of us who're waiting. They're directed back to their rooms upstairs.

I can barely keep my eyes open, but I know it's critical that I have my wits about me for all our sakes. No country likes foreigners killing off respected members of their populace.

It's forever before they indicate to Steve he's next.

"Remember what we discussed," I whisper as he passes where I sit with Andre.

Steve is gone a long while. When the police are finally finished with him, he heads upstairs. I shoot him a questioning look across the room. He grimaces and shrugs.

Next is Karista. She could be a wild card for us. Still in shock from the events on the yacht, she only half-listened as we outlined what we'd tell the police. One slip of Andre's name could cause his life to hang in the balance.

Karista exits after half an hour. With tears on her face, she hurries upstairs without glancing in our direction. I desperately want to leap past the police and ask her what she said.

Finally it's our turn. Andre and I are the only people left in the lobby. I insist on supporting him as we walk slowly down the hallway toward Vito's office.

"He's hurt and should be in bed," I tell the officer who's escorting us. He ignores me and ushers us to chairs in front of Vito's desk. It's uncomfortable remembering Francoise and the beggar sitting in these same seats so recently.

Only instead of Javier, two stern-looking officers sit opposite us. Both have the alert eyes and no-nonsense expressions of good policemen. They won't be easy to fool. The guest register is spread open in front of them.

But what surprises me the most is the sight of the older couple of guests I'd dubbed as "British." The woman with the flowered hats and the man who always wears Bermuda shorts and smokes a pipe. What are they doing here?

"Please sit and state your name," says the older of the

two Sumatran policemen.

"I'm Lexi Winslow and this man is Emerson Sawyer. He saved our lives. You can see he's been injured. He needs to be in bed. This no way to thank him for all he did," I start.

"Miss Winslow. We thank you for your phone call. We've spoken with Alfonso de Alevado. He spoke quite highly of you both and your assistance through this trouble."

Since Andre has a new identity and passport in the name of Emerson Sawyer, we all agreed that that's who he would be to the police. Andre hadn't mingled with the other guests much so there was no one to contradict him except for Ifrah. Alfonso swore her to secrecy and had Andre sign the guest register as Emerson, arriving a week ago. The guest known as Andre Van der Meer was documented as leaving before the storm struck. As there were no arrest warrants issued in the name of Emerson Sawyer, Andre will hopefully be safe—unless Karista said something different.

My hands start to tremble. Andre covers them by placing his hand on top of mine.

"We'd like to hear in your own words Mr. Sawyer, how you happened to be shot."

Andre says in a weak voice, "I saw the son of the hotel's owner and his men at the garage shooting at Lexi and her friends, Karista and Steve. I went to see what was going on and Javier's men just shot me.

The policeman looks over to the older couple. The man shrugs.

The policeman turns back to us. "Please continue."

I quickly interrupt. "Why are these hotel guests here?"

"My apologies. This is Sam Wilkes and Judy Prendergast. They work undercover for us. We've had suspicions about Vito de Alevado being involved with counterfeiting trade for some time."

He frowns at Sam and Judy. "They never suspected the equipment would be set up on the yacht."

Sam and Judy look embarrassed by the rebuke.

The policeman indicates for Andre to continue. As he talks, I think about Sam and Judy. They might realize Andre has been here longer than the register indicates. They may even have heard him called Andre. Not good.

Andre finally finishes telling them his version of our ordeal. He coughs and asks for water.

"And you, Miss Winslow," the policeman says. "Why were you taken to the yacht?"

"All I know is that Vito wanted names of our relatives in the States and to know how much ransom they could pay. Thank goodness Mr. Sawyer was with us. It was terrible with all those guns and men. I hope you put them all in jail.

"We can assure you that people are going to be incarcerated."

"May we go now? The doctor said Mr. Sawyer needs rest."

They ask a few more questions, but they seem to believe us.

I fish Fumiko's gold bracelet out of my pocket and place it on the desk. "Is this important? I found it outside Javier de Alevado's door. There's an inscription inside."

The policeman who hasn't spoken glances at the inscription. I can see he realizes what the inscription with Fumiko's name reveals. He looks up at me.

"Is that the Japanese woman that's been in the news?" I ask.

He nods.

"I wondered. Our bank received a notification about her disappearance." I add.

He passes the bracelet to Sam and Judy. He whispers to his partner.

I'm relieved, moments later, when we're finally excused with a parting comment. "We'll be verifying your story with your office in California. If we need more information, we'll contact you in the morning."

CHAPTER 32

It's dawn, but I'm too restless to sleep. Andre's fever broke a couple hours ago. He slumbers soundly now. We were so tired when the police finally dismissed us, we laid down on the bed without even taking our clothes off and fell asleep. I slip quietly from his side and step out on the hotel veranda. The morning air brushes my face with a clean caress. I savor the moment in spite of the chilly temperature. It's great to be alive.

The break in the weather continues, but even as I stand here, I can feel the wind picking up. The rain will probably be back by midday, but for now, the sun peeks through the gathering clouds.

If the police clear us, we'll be free to leave, although I won't feel safe until we're on a plane for the states. Who knows what the future holds for Andre and me, but last night I finally made a decision. Andre is my life. There's no question how I feel about him. Maybe there's a reason we're together other than the universe has a weird sense of humor. I'm going to quit worrying and enjoy the time we share. I only know that our relationship won't be a conventional one and whatever else, it won't be boring.

Out in the bay, I notice the police swarming all over the yacht. All that counterfeiting equipment and blank passports in the forward cabin will be pretty self explanatory. I wonder what they thought when they discovered the cofre room.

I see the two policemen who handled the interviews last night standing on the yacht's swim deck, talking with an officer who seems to be in charge. They move their arms up and down in agitation. Moments later they pause as a body bag is carried out of the yacht and loaded onto the police boat. It must be Javier. Sadly, his death won't bring back Denise or any of the other women he murdered, but at least there won't be any more.

I have one more thing to do this morning. I creep quietly down to the lobby ignoring all the antique knives and swords on the wall. With the help of a chair to stand on, I release the remaining caged birds. One by one, they realize they're free and fly away. It's a joy to see. Vito said he loved the birds, but some things aren't meant to be caged.

That's when I remember Cecilia back in Vito's office. Has anyone even fed or watered her for the last few days? I hasten to the office to find out.

There I find Alfonso sitting at Vito's desk with Cecilia perched on the back of his chair. The lines in his face tell it all. Last night must have been terrible for him. His son arrested and his grandson dead. His reputation in ruins.

"I'm so sorry," I say.

"They brought it upon themselves."

True, but I can see it doesn't lessen the pain. "Thank you for helping us."

He bobs his head wearily. "I apologize for what you went through at the hands of my family."

"What will you do with Cecilia?"

"You want to free her like you have all the other birds?"

"You knew?"

"I'm an old man and don't sleep well. I tend to rise early."

"But you didn't say anything."

"I agree wild things should be free, but I need you to leave me Cecilia. I'm afraid to let her go after all this time. She was raised from a small fledgling in captivity and is not likely to survive in the jungle. As the last of my line, Cecilia will keep me company in my old age."

He's right, of course. I wish him well and say my goodbyes.

Back upstairs, I slip quietly back into the Honeymoon Suite, still thinking about Alfonso.

"Cherie?" Andre calls from the bedroom. "Where have you been? Come back to bed."

I hurry in.

#

It's late by the time the four of us meet for breakfast. I notice Karista has moved her chair close to Steve.

"Did you get any sleep last night?" I ask them.

"Yeah, Andre's bed sure beat the couch," Steve says. "I brought Karista's stuff down from the third floor, so she didn't have to go back there."

"I felt safer taking the other bed in Andre's room with Steve nearby," she adds. "We were on the phone for a while with our parents."

Here comes the bad news. I'm fired. Somehow, my job isn't the most important thing on my mind. I know that will change when I get home, but right at this moment, I'm the happiest I've been in a long time.

Karista urges Steve, "Tell her."

"We still have our jobs. Karista's dad told mine that if we were fired, he'd remove all his money."

I'm overwhelmed. "Karista, Please thank your father. It means a lot to me."

No one feels much like talking after that, so we eat in quiet, each consumed with our own thoughts.

"How soon can we leave?" Karista asks.

Steve goes to check, He returns with good news. "The roads are clear. A small bus just arrived and is waiting to take guests to the airport. I arranged seats for us since there isn't any sign of the police."

The four of us rush upstairs and grab our things. Andre reappears with the canvas bag he carried from the yacht before the police arrived and a small suitcase. Curious, he hasn't let that tote bag far out of his hands since we left the yacht.

"Andre, what's in that bag?"

"Some personal items."

That could cover a multitude of things. "Promise me you didn't take anything from the cofre room."

"I did not."

"Honestly?"

He frowns. "I'm hurt you don't believe me. Would you like to look?"

"No," I say. "I'll take your word."

We climb on the bus, which fills quickly. Between the arrival of the monsoon season and the police, all the other guests are ready to leave, too. The driver stands in the front and counts passengers. He blocks the entrance when it's filled and tells the remaining guests that there will be another bus in an hour or so. Amid their groans, he climbs on board and takes his seat.

As I look out the window, a taxi arrives and a pompous-looking man in a dark suit and sunglasses jumps out and hurries into the hotel. The taxi makes a u-turn and leaves. That must have been an expensive fare, I think. Then I have a bad thought.

I rush up to the driver and whisper in his ear. "Get this bus moving now, and I'll pay you one hundred dollars

257

American."

He gives me a questioning look. "Immediately," I add, "or the deal's off. Don't let anyone else get on the bus." I pull a hundred dollar bill from my purse and hold it up.

Five seconds later, the driver rolls the bus out of the parking area. As we pass the entrance, the man from the taxi emerges. He waves frantically for the bus to stop. Someone must have told him we were on the bus.

Instead, the driver steps on the gas. I get a clear view of the man's angry, red face as we roll by.

He even chases us, banging loudly on the door to the bus. The driver stares straight ahead and increases our speed, leaving the man behind.

"What was that all about?" Andre asks.

"I think Clark of the FBI just arrived. I didn't feel like having a chat and missing our plane.

CHAPTER 33

I silently thank Kevin again as I settle back in my luxurious first-class plane seat. Karista and Steve are in the seats ahead. Andre naps next to me. He paid for his own seat through to Tokyo.

I finally feel safe. We've all been lucky to survive. Javier and his father were my first face-to-face encounters with serial killers. I've dealt with lots of nasty characters before, but none with as little regard for the lives of their victims. I'd rank Javier and Vito right there with Ted Bundy and Jeffrey Dahmer. I'll be very happy to return to the piranhas and little sharks that I usually hunt.

Getting through the airport in Medan was exhausting for Andre. It's hard to see a man as vital as Andre laid low. At least he's on the mend now. He shifts in his sleep beside me. His head lays on his canvas tote bag. I wonder again what's in it. I wish I'd looked when he made the offer.

I'm looking forward to going home. Contrary to what Steve thinks, I don't always live in my office. I miss my little apartment in Santa Monica. I can see the ocean from my balcony. With the windows open on a summer night, I can hear the sound of the waves. They help me sleep.

Still, I have torn emotions. We're all flying out of Sumatra to Tokyo. Andre will be leaving us there for parts unknown, because he's persona nongrata in the United States. He made arrangements for a friend to meet him when he deplanes. I wonder how long it will be before I see him again.

When Karista gets up and heads for the bathroom, I move forward and slide into her seat next to Steve.

"You know, there's a case in Brazil Howard has been after me to take on. Would you be interested? I could use some help."

"After all I did wrong on this trip? Wait, I thought you never worked with a partner?"

"Maybe I never had the right one before. Besides, I've almost got you broken in."

I don't mention I have ulterior motives because I don't want him to get a big head, but his people skills are invaluable since mine tend to be a bit abrasive. I think he could learn to be pretty good at this.

Steve practically leaps out of his seat. He's ecstatic.

"However, you will be taking a survival course as soon as we get home."

His happiness fades. "Wait. No more jungles, right?"

That's an appalling thought. "Not if I have anything to do with it." I say emphatically. "I feel like I owe you an explanation," I continue. "You remember when I told you about Andre? I left a small part out. During that job in Sydney, when we escaped for a weekend in Brisbane together, we got married."

"He's your husband?"

"I didn't know he was trying to con the countess out of the Rembrandt portrait of her great, great whatever grandmother. At the same time, I was having trouble locating the money the count stole from his nephew. So Andre and I spent a lot of time together. Three weeks later, we said our vows before a priest in a beautiful garden behind St. Catherine's. A month after that, the Rembrandt was gone and so was Andre."

"You never divorced?"

"I'm Catholic, you know. Not practicing, but I believe in for better or for worse. Besides, I was never sure what name to file a divorce in." Without thinking, my fingers rub my silver cross necklace.

"That's terrible." Steve says.

"If the police in the states ever discovered we were married, they would never have believed I didn't know about the Rembrandt he stole. I would have been locked up for sure as his accomplice."

Andre interrupts us from the seat behind us. "Are you going to tell him our entire life history? If so, don't forget to mention how you giggle in your sleep."

Steve scowls. I smile.

Karista comes back after a few minutes, and I return to my seat next to Andre. He takes my hand. "Andre is my real first name."

"And your real last name?"

"Is of no importance."

"Well at least I know you didn't marry me for my money."

Looking very serious, he leans over and whispers in my ear, "Cherie, that's what I've been trying to tell you for the past week. About our wedding, the minister, he, well, he wasn't exactly ordained."

I shake my head in disbelief. Such an old con and I totally fell for it. Andre could sell fleas to a dog.

I don't know how to react. Two years of my life thinking we were married. Not knowing what to do. Finally, the only reaction I have is to laugh at myself.

Andre's indignant. "Let's see you try to find a priest on Easter weekend. I couldn't. In the end, I refused to face letting you go, and I had to get the painting to Holland. Please, say you forgive me. We can get married in Tokyo if you'll lay over for a day."

"Your last proposal was more romantic."

"Please. I'm being serious."

"Say we do get married, what then? Every time you go out the door, I'd be afraid you won't come home. Or be arrested. Or worse, killed by some mysterious investor?

Are you ready to change careers for me?"

"I . . . I . . ." He's totally flustered.

#

I have difficulty letting go when I hug Andre goodbye in Tokyo. It seems like it's tough for him too. He slips something into my pocket and whispers in my ear, "This isn't the end for us. I love you. And I'll be back to convince you that I do."

As he deplanes, I notice he's holding that canvas bag close. Something in it must be very important to him. The bag hasn't left his hands since we boarded the hotel bus.

When he turns and blows me a kiss, I forget about the bag and blow him one back. How long will it be until we see each other again? I already miss him terribly.

As I watch his retreating back, I cry again. This time for a different reason.

"Goodbye, Andre."

Like the saying goes about releasing things you love, I can only hope he comes back. I'm just not sure what I'll do if he does.

I remember he put something in my pocket and retrieve it. It's a folded piece of paper. I open and read, If you ever need me, wire Andy Mergetroid c/o The Huntington Hotel, Monaco.

Mergetroid? Can that be his real name? Surely no one would make a name like that up.

I laugh. I can't help myself. What an awful time he

must have had at school. Poor Andre.

I clutch the note.

POSTSCRIPT

LAX Airport: A Month Later

The information board in the waiting area announces that the flight to Sao Paulo, Brazil leaves at 11:35 am.

I check my watch and turn to Steve. "It's half an hour until we board. I'm going to get a coffee. Want anything?"

Steve looks up from his book, A Guide To Brazil and shakes his head.

I make my way between the constant stream of travelers. When I reach the coffee shop, a newspaper left on a table catches my eye. I pause, stunned.

The front page of the paper shows a photo of the Goya from Vito's yacht and the headline reads: "New Found Goya Fetches Record Price In Japan for an anonymous seller."

The End

If you enjoyed *Land Sharks- A Swindle in Sumatra,*
please leave a review on Amazon.com

FORTHCOMING BOOKS

LAND SHARKS - BOOK TWO

Lexi, Steve, and Andre will be off on another
adventure soon.

For news about up-coming releases, please visit:
www.NancyRavenSmith.com or
www.Facebook.com/NancyRavenSmithWriter

COMING - SUMMER 2016

THE RELUCTANT FARMER OF WHIMSEY HILL

by
Bradford M Smith

with
Lynn Raven and Nancy Raven Smith

PRAISE - "Animals can and do make our lives better. This is my kind of book." Bret Witter, #1 New York Times Bestselling co-author of "DEWEY" (The Library Cat)

Here's a sample of *The Reluctant Farmer.*

PROLOGUE

HOW NOW BLACK COW

1971

If a black cow crosses your path, is it worse luck than a black cat?

I'm not a superstitious man. And yet, here I stand in the middle of the road about a mile away from our farm in rural Virginia wearing my best navy pinstriped suit.

Doesn't sound like such bad luck, does it?

But if this were a good news, bad news thing, that would actually be the good news. The bad news lies at the other end of the thick rope I'm clutching in my hands. That's where it circles the neck of a Black Angus steer named Pork Chop.

There's no doubt in my mind that this unruly beast was put on earth to torment me.

My family disavows all connection to Pork Chop. They refer to him as "my cow," as in, "Honey, your cow's out" or "Daddy, your cow needs to be fed." Somehow this animal has managed to alienate my entire family. Not an easy feat with a family as besotted and overrun with animals as mine is.

But for once, Pork Chop is not being rowdy. Actually, quite the opposite. He's lying on his side with all four feet stuck out stiffly. He looks dead, but he's just asleep. I can see his chest rising and falling steadily. Dead might be easier to deal with.

Judging by the long shadows cast by the nearby pine trees, it'll be dark soon. Pork Chop weighs nearly six hundred pounds, and there's no way I can move him on my own. As much as I'd like to, I can't leave him lying in the road to go for help. He could be injured or cause an accident. But if I don't go for help, who knows how long I'll be stuck here. Pork Chop isn't my family's favorite animal, yet they'll never speak to me again if he gets hurt.

A honk shatters the quiet. A neighbor slows down in his dusty, battered Ford pick-up. I raise my hand to wave him down. He waves back and drives on. I can see him snickering in the rear view mirror.

Our working farm neighbors don't know what to make of me. I'm still the outsider who works nine to five for the federal government.

I can understand their confusion. The country is not my habitat of choice. As a Boston native and a Cornell graduate with a Masters in Electrical Engineering, order, logic, and cleanliness matter to me. The robots I work with suit me perfectly. When I program them, they do what they're supposed to. Robots never pee, poop, bite, kick, or drag me where I don't want to go.

Unfortunately, my wife's animals do.

Learn more about *THE RELUCTANT FARMER* at
www.TheReluctantFarmerofWhimseyHill.com

Made in the USA
Las Vegas, NV
08 March 2021